"While our. . .houseguest is staying here, I want you to keep out of his way. He's not the kind of man I want my daughters consorting with."

That puzzled Hannah. Of all the young men she'd known, Eric seemed the least dangerous. One certainly couldn't accuse him of a life spent in dissipation—he'd probably only had acquaintance with the word when browsing through a dictionary. And she knew his economic status didn't matter— her parents had conceived this plan of moving into the rickety old farmhouse to take their children *away* from associating with the privileged class.

"I don't understand, Daddy." She voiced her confusion. "He seems like a nice man."

"Don't let appearances deceive you, Hannah. I don't trust him, and you'd be wise to follow my lead."

Hannah could barely believe what she was hearing. Eric had done nothing to merit disfavor. He'd done his utmost to seclude himself in his room, away from the family, at every opportunity. Hadn't her parents endlessly told her not to judge people for others' mistakes and to give second chances?

PAMELA GRIFFIN lives in Texas and divides her time among family, church activities, and writing. She fully gave her life to the Lord in 1988 after a rebellious young adulthood and owes the fact that she's still alive today to an all-loving, forgiving God and a mother who prayed that her wayward daughter would come "home." Pamela's main goal in writing Christian romance is to encourage others through entertaining stories that also heal the wounded spirit. Please visit Pamela at www.Pamela-Griffin.com.

Books by Pamela Griffin

In Search of Serenity

Pamela Griffin

Heartsong Presents

Thank you to my wonderful and faithful critique partners—my mother and my good friend Theo, both of whom are always there for me in a pinch. You are a blessing beyond compare.

Dedicated to my Lord and Savior, the God of second chances, of lasting redemption, of impossible reunions. And to all the families out there in need of these, this book is for you.

A note from the Author:
I love to hear from my readers! You may correspond with me by writing:

Pamela Griffin
Author Relations
PO Box 721
Uhrichsville, OH 44683

ISBN 978-1-61626-038-5

IN SEARCH OF SERENITY

All Scripture quotations are taken from the King James Version of the Bible.

All of the characters and events in this book are fictitious. Any resemblance to actual persons, living or dead, or to actual events is purely coincidental.

Our mission is to publish and distribute inspirational products offering exceptional value and biblical encouragement to the masses.

PRINTED IN THE U.S.A.

one

Before she could scream, a red-skinned man wearing hides and feathers clapped a hand over her mouth. With her back against the wall, she stared in horror. A sudden pounding shook the door of the cabin as whoever stood on the other side demanded entrance.

Would it be another wild man, such as the Sequoia who had come to raid her father's cabin, or one of the settlers, come to rescue her? Attempting to wrest free, she bit the hand of her captor and cried out at the top of her lungs for hel—

"Hannah!"

Hannah Thomas slashed a long *scrrritch* through the rest of the word, ripping through the paper with the nib of her pen. She compressed her lips in irritation.

"Hannah!"

"What *is* it, Abbie?" Hannah woefully eyed the ruined notepaper bearing the past hour of her hard labor.

"Mama wants you."

"And you had to tell me that, caterwauling my name at the top of your lungs as you raced into the parlor like a feline in a catfight?" Hannah eyed her little sister sternly.

"What's a feline?"

"A cat."

"I wanna be a bird instead."

"You're neither a bird nor a cat, but sometimes you act like a little wild Indian."

"Can I be the little Indian girl in your play? The one who makes friends with the collynith?"

"The colonist, and never mind. You're too young to remember all the lines."

"Am not!" Abbie crossed her arms over her chest with another pout that some thought cute but only irritated Hannah. A curious sparkle came into Abbie's eyes. "Whatcha writing?"

"Nothing." Hannah folded her hands over the ruined words as Abbie moved closer.

"Ooo—you're writing them shameful stories of intreak again! Mama said stories like that are sensatial claptrap. You shouldn't write them, Hannah."

"There's nothing shameful about my stories of *intrigue*, and they're far from being sensational claptrap. Anyhow, it's none of your business."

"I'm telling Mama you're being mean."

"I'm not being mean. I'm being truthful. And how do you know that I might not be working on the Founder's Day play?"

"If you were, you wouldn't have hid it from me."

Hannah blew out an exasperated breath. "Don't you have something to do? Dolls to play with or imaginary tea parties to hold?"

Abbie frowned. "They're not 'maginary. They're real."

"Fine. Go have one then."

"Can't. Mama said I have to go to bed."

"Good idea. Go back to bed."

"There's toys all over the top. And my bedsheet's all mussed up."

"Then pick them up. And straighten your sheets."

Abbie pouted. "I wish *we* had servants like Uncle Bernard does. How come we had to move to this dumb ole house, anyway?"

Hannah sympathized with her sister. She also had grown accustomed to being waited on during the five years they'd lived in her wealthy great-uncle's manor and didn't relish this new turn of events. Why her mother insisted that life at their great-uncle's wasn't beneficial for the children, Hannah couldn't understand. But Daddy had succumbed to Mother's wishes and bought the old Fairaday house for a song. Little wonder he'd acquired it so cheap. With the way it creaked and groaned, Hannah wondered if the place might be haunted by old Fairaday's ghost—perhaps his entire lineage.

And now her father was paying the price for his foolish mistake. What if it had been a ghost that caused him to fall from the roof, and not the sudden shock of hearing some wild animal chatter in a tree branch near his head? She wondered what kind of tale her pen could craft from that.

"Hannah!"

Her little sister's demand broke Hannah's imagination from spiraling down the latest path.

"How come we had to move?"

"I don't know, Abbie. But what's done is done."

"I don't like it here." Abbie stomped her bare foot. "I wanna go back to Uncle's. I want Mary to pick up my clothes and toys so I don't have to."

You and me both, kiddo. I don't like it here, either. She didn't air her futile thoughts, not wanting to set Abbie off on another tangent. "You just have to learn to make the best of things."

"I don't want to make the best of things. I *hate* this place!"

The doorbell rang, to Hannah's relief. She waited for the newcomer to be escorted into the parlor, thus putting an end to Abbie's complaints—then remembered they had no maid and she must answer the door herself. Mother was tending to Daddy, and Hannah's younger brothers and sisters were at school, where Abbie should be, if she hadn't come down with the sniffles and Mama hadn't sent her to bed. She certainly appeared recovered.

Hannah moved to receive their guest, then thought twice and grabbed up her notebook of loose-leaf papers. No sense putting temptation in Abbie's way, though she couldn't read well, not enough to understand the novel Hannah toiled over at every opportunity. But she didn't want to return to find her pages colored on, either.

Holding her story close to her heart, snippets of what she wrote revolved in her mind. Theatrically she wondered if the person on the opposite side of the door was indeed her rescuer. . .or a wild man come to wreak havoc.

The thumping of her heart increased as she opened the door. A stranger stood waiting. Taller than herself by at least half a foot, with wheat-colored hair and riveting blue eyes that reminded her of the bottom of a slow flame, the man took her breath away. His fair, patrician features could be described as romantic, even angelic, but the firm set of his jaw and intensity of his gaze beneath thick sable brows gave him the air of a rogue.

Wild man or rescuer?

It was difficult to tell from appearance alone.

She blinked, and he raised his brows. At that, she realized she'd been staring while holding her story clutched to her breast. "Can I help you?" she uttered breathlessly and pulled the notebook away. Unfortunately, she didn't have a good hold on the edges, and a shower of papers rushed to the ground between them. Still in a daze, she could only stare at the top of his hat and the broad girth of his shoulders outlined by the gray suit jacket he wore as he bent to retrieve the escaped pages of her story.

Surely, a rescuer. . .

Her face warmed as his gaze dropped to and remained on one of the papers in his hand—long enough to take a look at the first sentences, surely—but he didn't comment. She hoped he hadn't read any of it. He handed over the last sheaf of papers as he rose to stand. Again, she felt emotionally wrung by his intense blue gaze.

Perhaps a wild man. . .

Maybe both.

"Are you all right, mademoiselle?"

His voice, rich and warm, had the opposite effect and made her shiver.

"Yes, of course." Recalling that she still didn't know why he'd come to their ramshackle house, and figuring that in his herringbone suit with empty hands he didn't look like a salesman or a workman—not that her father would agree to hire one of those—she rephrased her question. "How may I help you?"

"Actually"—he gave her a smile that threatened to make her knees melt into goo—"I came here for your family."

"Pardon?"

"This is the Thomas residence?"

"Yes?" Her reply came wary.

"Then this is where I was told to come." He slipped his hand inside his coat. Alarmed, Hannah backed up a step, opening her eyes as wide as they would go. Surely, he wasn't going for his gun?

He drew his brows together in clear confusion, and she wondered if she'd gone white as a sheet. Clutching her notebook to her chest as if it were a shield of armor, she watched as he withdrew an envelope, her relief that it wasn't a weapon helping her marginally relax. She stared at the paper he handed her.

"It won't bite."

At his amused tone, she snapped out of her foolish trance. "What is it exactly?"

"I'm Eric Fontaine. . .and you weren't expecting me." The introduction he offered in calm confidence; the rest he added with uneasy knowledge.

"No, we weren't." His obvious embarrassment made her feel bad for him, also easing her anxiety. "The name is familiar though. Are you a friend of my father's?"

"My father and your father are old associates. My father sent me to help out. He heard about your father's accident.

It's all in the letter."

His explanation erased any lingering doubt about his character, and she took the envelope, offering him a smile and stepping aside to let him enter. "Please, come in. Father's upstairs. He's unable to leave his bed because he broke his leg, but then, I imagine you already know that if your father sent you." She closed the door behind him and led him to the parlor.

"I thought he would have phoned by now. I apologize for coming unannounced."

"Oh dear. There's one mystery solved. Our phone line isn't working. This place. . ." She gave a little shake of her head, spreading her hands in apology. "It's not in the best of shape on a good day, and—"

"Han-nah!"

She winced at Abbie's banshee yell and tried to cover her embarrassment with a short laugh. "My little sister. She stayed home from school because she had a smidgeon of a temperature. She's been restless all day."

"Han-nah!" Abbie shot around the corner and stopped in surprise to see their guest. "Who are you?"

Hannah sighed. "What do you want, Abbie?"

"Mama said you're to go up there right away."

"Oh right. I forgot." She turned to the man she wasn't yet sure how to classify, as friend or foe. Surely, if he came to help, he was their rescuer and not a rogue. "The parlor's through there. Make yourself comfortable—well, as comfortable as you can. The room's rather cold. It's certainly not the Ritz, not that I've been there. But, well, it's a wonder this place doesn't fall down around our heads. I'll just go give Father your letter. I'll be back shortly."

She bounced from one topic to another, as she often did when nervous or excited, then bit her tongue to prevent further rambling. With a parting nod, she exited the room. The moment she left his line of vision, she raced upstairs, too excited to share with her parents the news of their unexpected caller to walk at a more sedate pace.

⊷

Eric took a seat on the edge of a lumpy sofa, curbing the strong impulse to walk out the front door. The drafty house and uncomfortable surroundings didn't bother him; he was accustomed to sparser conditions. What made him ill at ease was the intent inspection he now received from the child who sat in a nightdress on a chair across from him, her legs too short for her bare feet to reach the ground as she swung them like small pendulums back and forth, back and forth. . . .

And stared.

He glanced away several times. He should be accustomed to children, but the unusual circumstances of his arrival put him on edge. He threaded the brim of his hat through his fingers.

"So," he said in an attempt to fill the uneasy silence, "your name is Abbie?"

A narrow-eyed nod was his reply.

"How old are you, Abbie?"

"Almost six."

"Really? I have a sister your age. Her name is Marguerite. We call her Merry, because she laughs a lot and likes to play games. Do you like to play games?"

This time her nod didn't seem as if it veiled a spitting kitten.

"Merry likes to hold tea parties. We run a mission, and sometimes she holds them with a few of our guests who've become like family."

A spark of reluctant curiosity lit her dark eyes. "What's a mission?"

"A place where people go to get help."

"Papa doesn't want no man's help. He said so."

Eric wondered just how welcome he would be at the Thomas residence. His father had led him to believe a pair of willing hands would be appreciated.

"Has your family lived here long?"

She shrugged. "I don't like this place. It smells funny. And nothing works right."

Eric withheld a smile, her little miseries reminding him of something his youngest brother might say. "Old houses do tend to have a musty odor. But what would you say if, assuming your daddy gives permission, I make things work right again?"

Curiosity warred with suspicion in her eyes. "How?"

"I have some experience fixing up old places."

"This place is really, really old."

He grinned. "I have experience with those places, too. The mission my family owns is really, really old."

For the first time, the girl smiled. "Are Merry's tea parties 'maginary?"

"Imaginary?"

"Like people in the stories Hannah writes."

"Ah." His smile grew. "No, I would have to say they're very real."

two

Hannah stood at the foot of her father's bed, curiously watching his face lose color, then flush darker as he read the letter. She wondered what Eric's father had written and almost wished she had slipped the contents from the envelope earlier, to see for herself.

Her father's lips thinned as he lowered the paper, his eyes lifting to Hannah. "He's downstairs?"

"Yes. I left him in the parlor."

"Tell him thanks, but we don't need his help."

"Bill, you must not speak so."

Her mother stood by his bedside, her bearing as regal as ever, her fluid voice soothing to hear after his terse words. Hannah often wished she could emulate her mother who behaved like the princess her name, Sarah, meant. But Hannah didn't come close, her behavior too strong-willed and animated to be compared to quiet aristocracy. Her great-grandfather may have been chieftain of his tribe on the island where her mother was born and lived the greater part of her life, as the only child of an island princess and an American missionary. Yet though such royalty existed in Hannah's bloodline, regrettably any outward manner of the nobles would never reign in Hannah.

"With winter soon here and your need of recuperation, any help this young man could give would be welcome," her mother continued quietly.

Her father glanced from her mother to Hannah, his manner furtive. Her mother followed suit and addressed her. "Hannah, please go downstairs and tell Mr. Fontaine that I'll be down shortly to receive him."

Disappointed to be dismissed yet again, she stubbornly hesitated. Why were so many secrets kept from her? What about the intriguing man downstairs did Hannah's father not want her to hear? At her mother's raised eyebrows, she whirled on her heel and left the room.

Seventeen years old and they still treated her as a child!

She brought the door to a close, losing her grip on the notebook. Her precious story fluttered to the floor. Aggravated, she bent to retrieve it, the door barely ajar. Her parents must not have heard the rustle of pages, for they resumed their conversation, unaware Hannah knelt close by.

"I won't have any son of *his* under my roof!" Her father used a harsh tone she'd rarely heard, except when events went beyond his control. Like when the doctor told him he must remain in bed several weeks to allow the break in his leg to heal.

"He told you he has changed when you last saw him," her mother replied in her quiet, logical way.

"That was over ten years ago! How do I know it's true? That he hasn't reverted to his old schemes and taught his offspring the same? What if this is all some huge con of Eric's for power or revenge? He was a master at manipulation. He knew tricks I'd never dreamed of."

"*You* have changed." The reminder was delivered gently. "Besides, what would he have to be vengeful of? You saved his life. He saved yours."

Stunned, Hannah stopped gathering papers. Eric Fontaine Sr. had saved her father's life? From whom? The Piccoli gang?

She knew little of her father's past—only that he'd been the target of a mobster long ago when he washed up on her mother's island. There, he found the Lord through Hannah's grandfather. But the mobster who had been pursuing him, Vittorio Piccoli, struck out in revenge against Hannah's father once he returned to America with his new wife, and as a result, her mother had almost died, like their child she'd been carrying. Those facts Hannah overheard one night, many years before, when all the children were thought to be in bed asleep and her parents were visiting with Uncle Brent and Aunt Darcy, Aunt Charleigh and Uncle Stewart. The adults had quietly been reliving the past after a few of them had gone to see Eric Sr. that day, having received the startling news of his proximity through a guest visiting the Refuge. Any other details regarding her father's life before Christ had been omitted from Hannah's curious knowledge.

Though she knew she shouldn't, she gathered the papers more slowly while craning her ear to the door, eager to hear more of the past she'd never known.

"Sarah, there's one thing I learned when it came to dealing with a man like Eric Fontaine, and that is the moment you begin to trust him is the moment you've put your life in jeopardy."

"Surely things are different now. He and his wife run a mission at the wharf for the destitute."

"I know. I remember what he told us: how he found God in prison and forgave Charleigh and Darcy for putting him there and is no longer out to seek vengeance." Her father's voice held an impatient edge. "But now I have to ask myself, was it all a cover? He was a master at getting anyone to believe anything. It was all part of his twisted genius."

"But again, Bill, what would he hold against you?"

"Maybe nothing. Doesn't matter. I don't want any son of Eric's near my girls."

All was quiet a moment.

"Could a man who delivered such a testimony as you have told me, years ago, when you and the others returned from visiting him, have a soul so black?"

"I don't know, Sarah. But I won't risk my family's lives by taking chances. Never again."

"Bill. . ." Hannah heard the mattress springs creak and

assumed her mother took a seat beside her father. "You're not to blame for what happened to me and our baby."

"If I had never gotten involved with the Piccolis—with men like Eric—that thug would have never shot you."

"Still you hold such guilt in your heart, my love?" The soft sound of a kiss came to Hannah. "You must release this torment. I want you to at last know peace."

"Pretty Sarah, you are everything to me. You, the children. . . I couldn't risk losing you again."

"Hannah?"

At the sound of her sister's voice, Hannah jumped so sharply she almost fell through the door. She just stopped herself, slapping her palm to the wall. Certain now her parents must know she'd been eavesdropping, she scampered up off her knees, papers retrieved, and hurried down the hall to where Esther stood.

"What are you doing here? Were you spying on me?"

"Me, spying?" Esther scowled in disbelief. "I wasn't the one on my hands and knees crawling around in front of Mama and Daddy's door. Who's the suave fellah in the parlor?"

"No one that need concern you. Are you skipping classes?"

"It's past three, birdbrain."

Hannah sighed. "I had no idea it was so late. Come downstairs. Where's David?"

"Probably in the kitchen, stuffing his face with milk and cookies."

Her thirteen-year-old sister seemed to be in as disagreeable a mood as Abbie.

"Bad day at school?" she sympathized.

Esther shrugged. "The same. . ."

"But?" Hannah took her sister's arm, turning her around to walk with her as she began to descend the stairs. She expected her parents' door to open any moment and her mother to catch her lurking there.

Esther let out a frustrated sigh. "Betty and Claudia wanted

to come over and work on a report the teacher gave. I told them no, of course. I wouldn't *dream* of letting them see this hovel. Not after them seeing the grandeur of Great-Uncle's manor!"

Hannah understood implicitly. Betty and Claudia were the young sisters of two of her own friends, Julia and Muffy. The mayor's daughter and a judge's daughter. She had yet to surrender to their persistent requests for Hannah's new address and feared she would soon run out of excuses.

"Never mind that now," Hannah instructed. "Be on your best behavior."

Esther nodded at the familiar rule enforced at her great-uncle's mansion and which her family had carried on. When guests were present in the home, frowns altered into smiles, however false, and current troubles were conveniently swept under the carpet until they had the house to themselves again. In short, they put on a grand act. Hannah only hoped her baby sister had finally learned that rule and wondered about her choice to leave Abbie alone with their guest.

Had Abbie aired all the family secrets by now?

What rare secrets the children knew.

Hannah moved with Esther into the parlor, relieved to hear Abbie tell Eric of her intricate doll collection. Their childless great-uncle had brought her a doll from every country he'd visited while on business, and they'd become Abbie's frequent tea party guests.

At Hannah's approach, Eric turned her way. Her heart gave that unexpected lurch again.

"Mother will be down presently." She felt surprised her voice came out naturally when he looked at her with those blue, blue eyes. "May I bring you something to drink?" She winced, realizing she should have asked before she'd gone upstairs. Her great-uncle's maid usually took care of such trivialities. "We have coffee that Mother put on earlier."

"We have lemonade, too!" Abbie put in enthusiastically.

"I'll have some of that. *Merci*."

Eric smiled, and Hannah felt the now familiar *thump-thump* hammering in her chest before she whirled on her heel and hurried for the kitchen. *Oh my, he speaks French, too?* Once she retrieved his lemonade and returned to the parlor, she noticed her mother had joined him.

"My husband and I wish to extend our thanks for your offer of help."

Hannah's stomach dipped as she handed Eric the glass. Her mother's tone didn't bode well.

"As you know, he's incapacitated at the moment and unable to come downstairs to speak with you. He's expressed a desire for you to come upstairs and meet with him, instead."

Hannah blinked. From what she'd heard of her parents' conversation, she had expected Eric would be given the bum's rush. Not an invitation for a meeting.

"Of course." He took a sip of lemonade and set it down on the end table.

"Hannah, dear, will you start dinner?"

Disappointed that she couldn't tag along, she gave a short nod. If she hurried, she might be able to catch the tail end of their conversation.

❧

Eric followed the stately woman up the split staircase. Pictures of flower arrangements had been used to cover the worst water stains on the faded wallpaper, and when Mrs. Thomas switched it on, the electrical light flickered on the landing.

"The wiring up here is an abysmal mess. Please, watch your step."

As he walked, Eric's calculating mind took note of repairs needed, along with an educated guess of how long it would take to accomplish each task. She led him through a door at the east end of the house with a huge window that would let in the morning sun. This room, at a glance, appeared in better condition than what he'd seen of the rest of the place.

"*Good. . .night!*"

At the slow exclamation of profound shock, Eric looked toward the large bed and its occupant, who'd spoken. Mr. Thomas lay with his leg in a cast, his shoulders powerful and body lean—clearly an outdoorsman. His manner was reminiscent of a lion that had been caged for an eternity. He had hair a shade darker than Eric's with graying sideburns, a smattering of whiskers, and intense, light blue eyes that burned a hole through Eric.

"If I didn't know better, I could swear time rolled back twenty years." Mr. Thomas pushed himself up on his palms so he sat upright against the mountain of pillows at his back. "You're the spitting image of your father."

"So I've been told, sir." The manner in which the man offered the remark didn't resemble a compliment, and Eric refrained from saying more.

"So he sent you all the way to Connecticut to help us."

"Yes, sir."

The man took him in from head to toe. "What experience have you had with home renovations?"

"My family runs a soup kitchen, as you know. All of us have learned to be industrious in repairs. One of my uncles is a building contractor, and I also have some experience with electrical wiring."

At this revelation, Mrs. Thomas smiled hopefully.

"Why should Eric send you? How'd he learn about my accident? I haven't spoken with him in years."

"My father mentioned he owed you a great debt and asked if I'd be willing to help. As for how he found out, I don't know." His father had contacts everywhere. Through the years, his knowledge of others and of their business had been commonly acknowledged fact—and its sources had remained secret. As a result, Eric and his siblings were never able to get away with anything as children. Their shrewd father had always been one step ahead of any mischief.

"Humph. Shouldn't be surprised. Eric always did have a knack for figuring things out." Mr. Thomas's words reflected Eric's thoughts. "You sound well educated." His tone matched the skepticism in his eyes.

"Yes, sir. I took a year's schooling at our local university."

"Really? A college education yet? Makes one wonder why you do your own home repairs," he scoffed.

"Bill," his wife gently reproved.

"You haven't got a job elsewhere?"

"*Non.* I've spent most of my time helping out at the mission."

"To run a place like that seems as if it would incur a great deal of expense. Your father must have a lot of money."

"Bill, please." His wife again spoke softly, putting her hand to his shoulder as if to restrain him, and Mr. Thomas briefly shut his eyes.

"We get by." Outwardly, Eric remained unflappable. The man's thinly veiled accusations brought to mind just how his father had gained some of the money, stolen in his youth, but all of it now put to a worthy cause. His maternal grandfather had also left a sizable sum to Eric's mother before he passed away, and they received donations for the mission. The majority of financial help had dwindled with the crash of the stock market and the ensuing Great Depression.

Mr. Thomas continued to eye Eric as though he might suddenly abscond with the family silver and make a mad dash for the door. Eric tried not to feel offended. His father had warned him that being his son and a replica of his appearance, those from Eric Sr.'s past might be suspicious of his character, though Eric Jr. hadn't guessed they would be outright rude. He had offered to help them without compensation, for pity's sake!

No one from his father's past lived near the mission, or if any did, no one visited, save for that one time over a decade ago. Eric had been a small boy then, barely able to recall this man and others coming to see his father about former days, involving a stolen diamond necklace that passed through many hands. Affable by nature, never having had difficulty making friends, Eric now found himself for the first time regarded with great suspicion.

"Where are you staying?"

Even that question was delivered with wariness.

"I haven't found a place. I was hoping you might recommend somewhere I can board, as I'm not familiar with your town."

"Humph." His interrogator snorted a disgruntled reply. "Good luck finding a room."

"My husband's correct," Mrs. Thomas said pensively. "What is made available is ridiculously steep in price. But if you should come work for us, I wouldn't feel comfortable with you giving of your time and receiving nothing in return. We will give you room and board."

"Sarah?" Mr. Thomas gave her a bug-eyed look, his mouth agape.

She offered him an apologetic glance then again looked at Eric. "Would you excuse us for a moment?"

"Of course. I'll just step outside."

Once in the corridor, even after shutting the door, he could hear their faint words.

"It is only right, Bill. And we need the help. With Josiah away at school and David too young to mastermind any project, we need someone capable to take on such a load. The roof leaks, the walls need to be patched, and soon the snows will come. If we cannot get the house ready by winter, I fear we will need to move back to the mansion. And that can be detrimental, especially for the children. You've seen how they've become. Self-centered. Snobbish. With no concept of what is of true value. I was wrong to beg you to let us stay with Uncle Bernard all those years ago. I better understand now the rift between Uncle and Father. Uncle's ideals are shallow, and his concept of Christianity so ungodly. . . . I only pray it's not to late to save our children."

"Sarah, it's not your fault. I understood your desire to want to get to know your only other living relative, and I wanted to make you happy by staying there. As the children's father, I should have realized what that lifestyle was doing to them. I should have made the decision to move us out earlier. Maybe I should have quit working for him, but with the way the economy is and so many mouths to feed, it wouldn't be wise—though after so much time away, I wonder if I'll still have a job there."

"My uncle would be a fool to let you go, as much help as you've been to him. The situation's not your fault, either. You've always done what is best for the children and me. But Bill, what does it say for us if we shun this young man and judge him for what he cannot help being—Eric's son? We taught the children not to judge rashly and never on outward appearances alone."

Mr. Thomas grumbled something Eric couldn't make out.

"Yes, he *is* Eric's son, but he's also honorable. I sense this about him."

"On one meeting alone?" Her husband's tone soared in disbelief.

"I think we should give him a chance."

"You're far too trusting, Sarah."

"And you're filled with too much mistrust. I know this is because of your former life as a criminal. But darling, he isn't going to murder us in our beds."

"How can you be so sure?"

"Any man who forfeits his college education to help his parents run a soup kitchen for the needy doesn't strike me as someone so selfish that he would seek to harm others."

It was a moment before he replied.

"I still don't like the idea of him in our home, but I can't fight such logic, and you're right about one thing: We need the help since I'm laid up and no good to anyone right now."

"That's not true. Without you, I would fall apart."

"Truth be told, pretty Sarah, you're the glue that holds this family together. But just so you know, I'll be keeping an eye on him. First sign of trouble, he's out the door. I want a record of what he does every minute of the day. And warn the girls to stay away from him."

"Yes, my love. I will do all you ask."

All went quiet, leaving Eric to his thoughts.

If he was smart, he'd just walk out that door Mr. Thomas had threatened to throw him out of. But he couldn't. He'd made a promise to his father.

A rapid tread on the stairwell brought his attention to the landing. The lovely brunette he'd met earlier raced up them. Her short hair bounced with her steps. Upon reaching the landing, she caught sight of Eric and abruptly came to a stop, her cheeks flushing a pretty rose.

"Oh! Hello. . ." She glanced at her parents' closed door then back at him.

"The jury's still out," he explained.

"I see." Her face cleared, and she smiled. "Did Daddy seem. . .agreeable?"

"Let's just say he wasn't happy with the prospect of having me for a houseguest."

Her big, almond-shaped eyes opened wider. "Houseguest?"

"Your mother extended an invitation for me to room here while I fix up the place."

The door suddenly opened, and Mrs. Thomas appeared. She looked from Eric to her daughter, her eyes filled with clear question to see her there. "Hannah?"

"I went to light the range, but we're out of matches."

"Oh dear. I don't think there are any more in the house."

Eric pulled a matchbook from his pocket. "Here. Use this."

The older woman's eyebrows went up in surprise then sailed even higher when she saw the name of a nightclub inscribed on the paper flap.

"You don't smoke or drink?" she asked worriedly.

"No. Before I left, Father wanted to give me the number to your home in case I couldn't find it. We didn't have paper handy, and one of the visitors at the mission had this on him. Father wrote it down. There." He felt ill at ease as he pointed out the numbers penned inside. Of all the idiotic things to do. He already wavered at the edge of their decency list. Producing a matchbook that advertised a New York nightclub wasn't going to win him approval.

"Yes, well, all right." Mrs. Thomas smiled faintly and handed the matches over to her daughter. "Start a pot of water to boil for noodles. I'll be down shortly."

"Yes, Mama." Hannah offered Eric another shy, friendly smile and moved back downstairs.

"My husband and I have agreed you should stay. We are both grateful for whatever help you can offer."

Eric thanked her, tending to believe Hannah's mother was the only one with any true gratitude.

"You may have the room we plan for Josiah to use when he comes home on Christmas break." She walked with him past several closed doors he assumed opened into other bedrooms and turned the glass doorknob of a room at the end of the corridor, where a window stood. Before following her inside, he glanced out the spotted pane, noticing that here, too, a rich panorama of maples, firs, elms, and oaks grew in abundance. A vivid array of brightly hued leaves covered the grounds.

Two windows brought light into a musty room with a stately, four-poster bed and dark furnishings. A bureau held more drawers than he would need.

"The dust has collected," she apologized. "I'll tidy and make up your bed with fresh linens."

"You don't have to do that—"

"Nonsense. If you would like, you may relax here before dinner. The lavatory is across the hall."

He smiled, warming to the woman. "I came here to help *you*."

She chuckled in disbelief. "Surely you don't plan to start work now?"

"Whenever you need me."

"Rest tonight. I imagine it was a long trip from New York. I remember how tedious train travel can be."

He nodded. "All right. I'll just go collect my things. I left them outside." He had set his duffel bag at the end of the stoop, out of sight and hidden by shrubbery, having felt odd to appear at their door with luggage in hand.

She smiled kindly. "Dinner is at seven. And please, Mr. Fontaine, during your stay with us, consider our home yours."

What benevolence her husband lacked, Sarah Thomas made up for in spades.

He thanked her and went downstairs to collect his bag. Outside, he bent down to grab it.

"My, my, my," a feminine purr came from behind. "What have we here?"

three

With the stove lit and noodles simmering, Hannah smoothed her skirts and left the kitchen.

She glanced into the parlor.

Empty.

Where was Eric? Still upstairs?

She cast a curious glance up the staircase just as the front door opened.

Her heart jumped at the sight of him then fell when she noticed her two visitors.

"Julia! Muffy!" She hoped they couldn't see her dismay. "What are you doing here?"

"You were so secretive about your new home, we just couldn't help ourselves." The look in Julia's eyes as she studied the foyer made her disapproval clear. Hannah was surprised she didn't swipe her manicured finger along the entry table to check for dust.

"No wonder you didn't invite us over, you naughty girl." Muffy glanced at Eric, squeezing his arm. "Clearly you've been keeping secrets!"

Eric smiled at Hannah's friend. "If you ladies will excuse me, I'll be going to my room." He took the stairs.

"His *room*?" Muffy's eyes grew round. "So what is he, Hannah? A distant cousin? A friend of your brother's?"

"Actually, he's here to help out."

"Help out?"

She watched Eric reach the top landing, feeling a sting of rejection that he'd ignored her when earlier he'd been most attentive. "He's working for my father."

"Do tell!" Muffy grabbed Hannah's arm eagerly.

"Your father certainly picked a. . .distinctive house to purchase." The condescension fairly dripped off Julia's words. "So much different from your great-uncle's beautiful manor."

Embarrassment brought a surge of heat to Hannah's face.

"Yes, it certainly is different." With Eric gone, Muffy took notice of her surroundings for the first time.

Hannah's mother descended the stairs. She nodded in distant greeting. "Girls."

"Mrs. Thomas." Julia's attitude underwent a dramatic change. "What a lovely home you have."

Her mother's smile seemed frosty. "I hadn't realized you were having guests for dinner, Hannah."

"They just popped in for a minute."

"Oh yes," Julia agreed with a syrupy smile. "We were on our way to that divine new little boutique and dropped by to invite Hannah. My sister mentioned where you now live, and Muffy and I were eager to see your charming home for ourselves."

"Really." Her mother's aloofly polite manner didn't alter. "It's rather late for a trip into town. You wouldn't be back before nightfall, surely, and we've not yet had dinner."

"Yes, well. . ." Julia seemed a bit taken aback and grabbed Muffy's arm. "We'll just be going then. We should hurry before the boutique closes. We'll call you, Hannah."

Hannah refrained from mentioning that they didn't yet have a working phone, still mortified that her elite friends had seen her deprived set of circumstances. And, oh dear! She stood there wearing an *apron* of all things! Like a servant! Hurriedly, she whipped it off—though they might not have noticed her poor state of dress at all, after spending all their time gawking at Eric and the sad condition of the foyer.

Both girls had already turned for the door.

Her mother, however, noticed her flustered action and regarded her with a raised brow once they were alone. "You know how I feel about your spending time with those girls,

Hannah. It was bad enough when you attended the ladies' academy with them."

"I didn't ask them to come, Mother."

She nodded with a slight smile, her tension easing. "Come, help me and Esther with dinner, dear. Together we will master this art of cooking, no?" Hannah followed her to the kitchen, and her mother continued, "Cooking with a stove is much different from cooking over an open flame as I did on the island."

"Perhaps we should hire a chef," Hannah suggested hopefully. "Especially since we have a guest staying with us."

Her mother turned from collecting eggs from the icebox and gave her a level look. "Money isn't the answer to all problems in life."

"But it helps—"

"We will get by without servants. It will be a challenge, but a good one. You'll see."

"Yes, Mama," Hannah replied with scant enthusiasm.

Together, they prepared eggs and noodles, and Hannah sliced bread. Esther remained quiet but sullen as she set plates and silverware on the table. Abbie wandered in, still in her nightgown. "I wanna help."

Their mother shook her head. "You should be in bed."

"I feel fine, Mama. I'll pour the tea."

"No, Abbie—"

But Abbie had already lifted the full pitcher over a glass. The lip of it fell onto the edge, knocking the glass over. Tea rushed in a torrent over the table and nearest plate, also soaking Abbie's gown and splashing Esther.

"Abbie!" Esther wailed, grabbing a napkin. "Now see what you've done!"

"I'm sorry." Tears glazed Abbie's eyes as she set the pitcher down. "I didn' mean to."

"You can't do anything right! You're such a big baby!"

"Esther, that's enough," their mother scolded. "Abbie, you

must learn to mind. Now go change into another nightgown and get back into bed."

Hannah glanced at Abbie's crestfallen expression, feeling a twinge of sympathy. "I'll take her, Mother."

"Yes, do. And please tell Mr. Fontaine that dinner is ready."

Hannah took her little sister's hand and went with her upstairs. In Abbie's room, she helped her change into dry clothing, tucked the child into bed, and pulled the sheets beneath her chin. Feeling remorseful for having lashed out at Abbie before Eric's arrival, she brushed the girl's curls from her forehead. "Don't feel bad, sweetheart. Accidents happen."

"I can't do anything right," Abbie moaned. "And nobody ever lets me try."

Hannah smiled. "Oh, that won't last forever. You're only five."

"Almost six!"

"Yes, all right, never mind. Get some sleep. Things will look brighter in the morning."

"I'm hungry."

"I'll bring you a plate."

Abbie crossed her arms over her chest and pouted, clearly not happy to be stuck in her room. Hannah departed, leaving the small lamp by the bedside lit.

She spotted their guest standing with his arms crossed and looking out the window that stood at the corridor's end.

With her heart fluttering, Hannah approached, noticing how the waning daylight boldly framed his lean physique and brought it into clear view. His coat now absent, Eric wearing only a white shirt and dark trousers, she took in the broad length of his shoulders and back that tapered to a narrow waist, slim hips, and long legs. Clearly whatever work he did at their family's mission kept him in fine form.

Feeling a sudden rush of weakness, she swallowed hard.

Perhaps, a wild man after all. . .

"Mr. Fontaine?"

He turned and looked at her. Since he wasn't wearing his hat, she more easily noticed the slight curl to his thick hair.

"Um, Mother asked me to tell you that dinner is ready."

"Merci. I'll be down shortly." He turned back to the window.

"All right. . ." Confused, she hesitated then walked away.

Why did it seem that he wished to avoid her?

❧

Dinner with the Thomases was nothing like the circus at home, with Eric's nine siblings often all talking at once to be heard. The youngest girl, Abbie, was absent; Hannah's sister Esther acted sullen; and their little brother, David, stared at Eric across the table with blatant curiosity. But for all that, they executed proper table etiquette he'd never seen in children so young. He sensed Hannah's frequent glances but didn't look at her. In the conversation he'd overheard, Hannah's father had made it clear Eric was to have no association with his daughters. He had no wish to cause problems, and he wasn't here to make friends. He would do the job he came to do then return home to New York.

"Tell us what life is like where you come from, Mr. Fontaine," Hannah spoke suddenly.

He glanced at her then away. "We live near the wharf. Our home is split in half: the back part housing our family and the front part the soup kitchen. Basically, it's a huge room with nothing but tables and chairs and a few cots by the wall for those in need of a place to sleep for the night—though Mother has taken a few into our home on occasion."

"Really?" Esther's eyes bulged. "You take bums off the street into your *house*?"

"Esther," her mother said in low reprimand.

The girl's eyes lowered to her plate.

"Mother has a very generous heart," Eric explained. "There have been times when she's given one of my sister's beds to a destitute woman in need—often a runaway or a child thrown out of her parents' home."

Hannah gasped. "People do that? Throw their children out on the streets? I thought that was just in fiction, like in the movies."

Eric regarded her in disbelief. Where had she been the last several years? Didn't she see the effects that the depressed economy had wrought on so many lives?

"Your mother sounds like a wonderful woman," Mrs. Thomas said with a smile. "And your father—he also helps with the mission?"

He recognized her careful question to gain more information. Under the circumstances, he didn't blame her. "Mother is the heart of the mission, but Father is the soul. He runs the place practically single-handed. He makes a real difference. The difference of hundreds of people not starving. Of making sure that each night everyone who needs it has a hot meal. He treats every man, woman, and child as if they're a guest, not a liability, and cares about each one of them."

He realized he was getting a little too aggressive in pointing out his father's finer qualities and calmed, taking a sip of tea.

"He sounds like a wonderful man." Mrs. Thomas's voice became soothing. "I admire those who sacrifice their needs to put others first, just as our Lord did when He walked the earth."

He smiled at the genteel lady, whose bearing reminded him of benign royalty.

During the remainder of the meal, he fielded more questions about his family from the children, especially regarding his siblings. When Mrs. Thomas brought out a pie for dessert, less tension prickled in the atmosphere than when he'd first sat down.

"I bought this at the bakery." Her words sounded like an apology. "I still haven't learned how to master the oven."

Eric regarded her with a curious smile. "We don't have pies, except at Christmas, so it will be a treat."

David looked at him as if he'd come from a foreign country. "Golly, that's awful. We had dessert every night when we lived at Uncle's. Wish we could go back. This place is dumb."

"David." His mother eyed him sternly. "Language. And we must be thankful for what the Lord has provided. I have long prayed that we could live together under one roof as a family."

"I think maybe you should've prayed harder, Mama. 'Cause this roof leaks."

"Weren't we a family at Uncle's?" Esther insisted.

Mrs. Thomas glanced Eric's way, as if in apology, then at her daughter. "We will discuss this another time."

Eric pondered the children's words. Clearly they lived an affluent life before moving. But this huge house with its many rooms could hardly be called one of poverty. What must it be like to have servants take over the most basic of tasks? And what had caused them to leave such a pampered existence? It seemed a useless sort of life, and he felt sorry they'd missed out on the experience of real living up until now.

He found his gaze wandering to Hannah. She used her fork to flake away her piecrust, showing little interest in eating it. She frowned suddenly, then lifted her gaze to his. He inhaled a swift breath, as he looked into her eyes, huge, like those of a doe, but blue-gray in color.

Looking away, he thanked Mrs. Thomas for the meal and excused himself from the table.

Upstairs in his room, he prepared for bed. He had just tied a robe around his pajamas when a light knock sounded on the door. He opened it, surprised to see Hannah. She blinked, taking him in from head to foot.

"You're not going to retire?" she asked in shock.

"It's going on eight thirty."

"Exactly. I thought perhaps you might like to play a game of cards or listen to the radio."

"Thanks, no. If I want to rise before dawn, I should go to bed."

"Before *dawn*?"

At her stunned response, he felt it necessary to ask, "What time do you and your family usually get up?" He didn't want his hammering to wake anyone.

"Mama is up before any of us. I often sleep 'til noon, and so do the others on weekends."

"Noon?" He shook his head in disbelief. He would obviously have to wait on roof repairs and would inspect the lower floor until then. "I appreciate your letting me know. I'll be as quiet as I can."

She appeared at a loss for words. "Well, I suppose there's nothing else. . . . Do you have everything you need?"

"Your mother took care of that earlier."

"Oh. Well, then. Good night."

"Good night."

Eric closed the door, wondering if he'd misread her quiet disappointment.

Minutes later, he found it difficult to concentrate on the scripture passage he'd chosen before retiring, his thoughts centered on this odd family and one member in particular. Recalling a pair of large doe eyes shining up at him with expectation, he closed the book and crawled into bed, dousing the light. He wished he could douse the image of her in his mind as easily. He got the distinct impression that his need to create distance would soon be challenged.

four

Hannah awoke and blinked at her clock. Ten o'clock? Thoughts of their houseguest had made it difficult to sleep; she'd been unable to think of little else but Eric and felt surprised at the earliness of the hour.

She dressed and hurried downstairs. There was no sign of their guest, and she stifled a rush of disappointment. She poured herself a cup of coffee from the pot on the stove and took a bagel from the bakery box. Had they been at her great-uncle's, she would have indulged in a four-course breakfast the servants prepared. But stuck with the task of making her own, she decided to dispense with it altogether.

She found Eric in the parlor, pulling back frayed paper to inspect the walls. He turned at her step. "Good. You're up. I need to work on the roof."

"So soon?" she blurted, not wanting him to leave the moment she walked inside.

"I've lost a good four hours of daylight. If you could tell me where your father's tools are? I didn't bring my own."

"I imagine he put them in the shed out back."

He nodded and began to walk away.

"Will you—will you be wanting lunch?"

He looked at her strangely. "You eat lunch this early?"

"No, of course not." Flustered, she tried to think. "I just wanted to know if you would be wanting any." Her words sounded inane, and she wished she could erase the last few minutes and start over again.

He stared as if not sure what to make of her. "Just call me when it's ready."

He disappeared out the door, and she released an aggravated

breath. "Fine." Clearly he wanted little to do with her. What had she done to make him lose interest so quickly? He had been so charming when he first arrived, quickly swooping to her rescue when she dropped her story.

Thinking of her manuscript, she sighed and went to the library. Standing on a chair, she pulled her notebook from its hiding place on a top shelf. Abbie would never think to look there, and Hannah's room contained no true area of concealment.

She was well into the third chapter when the doorbell rang.

Reluctant to quit, she set down her pen and answered the door. Her stomach dropped when she saw her guests.

"Bet you didn't think you'd see us again so soon," Muffy gushed as both she and Julia practically shouldered their way past Hannah into the shabby foyer. "We have so much to discuss, but first, where is your simply divine houseguest?" Muffy eagerly looked around the area. "He is such a sheik!"

Hannah's face flamed with embarrassment at Muffy's effusive words and the disparaging glance that Julia offered the stained, papered walls.

"This is quite a. . .fascinating little place your father found." The adjective came across as *condemned* and *horrid*, befitting a poorhouse.

The two girls moved farther inside without invitation. "Does this. . .place. . .have a parlor?" Julia asked in polite disdain.

Hannah felt surprised the mayor's daughter would condescend to remain. "Of course. But Mother might not wish me to entertain company today." She never understood her mother's antipathy toward her socialite friends, whose esteem she'd worked so hard to win, but at this moment, she shared her mother's desire to have them gone.

"Silly Billy." Muffy grabbed her arm. "Did you forget we're part of the theatrical committee for the presentation?"

"But that's a few months away."

"My mother wants to ensure that all goes smoothly." Julia took the lead as if she knew every room in the old house.

Hannah hurried ahead, thankful that the library, at least, wasn't in as terrible a condition as the other rooms. "I have the information in here."

Julia's assessing glance of the library could hardly be called accommodating, but Hannah had new problems when she caught sight of Eric walking past.

"There you are!" Muffy practically squealed and rushed into the corridor to snag his arm and pull him inside. "You naughty boy, you're not avoiding us, are you? Where are you off to in such a hurry? The gymnasium? I've never seen such muscles. Tell me, do you lift barbells, too?"

Eric glanced at Hannah, and she winced with embarrassment at Muffy's behavior. He wore no suit coat or tie; his shirtsleeves rolled past his elbows exposed skin baked golden by the sun. His exertions had caused his shirt to cling to his strong physique, and the ends of his hair curled from dampness. Hannah swallowed and put her hand to the desk to support her suddenly weak limbs. Deciding it would be wiser to take a chair, she sat down. Eric looked away from her and smiled at Muffy.

"No, mademoiselle. Just hard, honest labor."

"*Mademoiselle?*" Muffy glanced at Hannah, never letting go of Eric. "He's French? Oh, tell me where you found him. He's just too scrumptious for words!"

"Are you from this area?" Julia's words were almost a purr as she moved with feline grace toward him. "I don't recall seeing you at any society functions."

"I'm from New York."

"New York!" Muffy responded as if the state were on the other side of the world instead of a few hours away by train. "Not that I'm complaining, but whatever are you doing in our small community?" She sidled closer to him.

With a frown, Hannah noticed Eric didn't pull away, didn't even try.

"Eric Fontaine is the son of an old associate of my father's," Hannah explained. "Eric, these are my friends, Muffy and Julia."

"Oh, this is intriguing," Muffy gushed again, smiling up at him. "And Eric is so powerful a name."

Hannah wanted to groan at Muffy's display, wanted to push her out the door and tell both girls to leave her father's pathetic old house.

"So have you come for a visit?" Julia's eyes also shone with interest, looking him up and down as a possible new conquest. She had a habit of acquiring and disposing of beaus whenever she suffered a case of ennui.

"Actually, I've come to help the Thomases."

"Help them?" Muffy looked back and forth from Hannah to Eric in curiosity, as if she'd forgotten Hannah had stated the same thing the previous day.

"I've come to help with repairs on the house."

"You're a handyman?" Julia's eyes widened.

"In this case, yes. If you'll excuse me, ladies. . ."

"I'll call you when lunch is ready," Hannah said before he could leave, perturbed that except for one initial glance in her direction, he had ignored her since entering the room.

"Lunch?" Muffy huffed a little laugh in disbelief. "It's gone past three, dear."

"Past three?" Hannah had been so involved in writing she hadn't realized how much time had elapsed. Her mother must have left the house, not to call them to the meal. "I'm so sorry. . ."

He shrugged. "I found an apple. Ladies, if you'll excuse me." He smiled at her friends, again ignoring Hannah.

"Must you go?" Muffy asked.

"*Oui*, I have a lot of work to finish before sundown."

"My, my. . .a real man. . .off to toil in the great outdoors."

Hannah couldn't be sure if Julia's reply sounded intrigued or insulting.

"I'll call you when dinner's ready then," Hannah called out after him.

He directed the barest of glances her way, without the smile he'd given the others. "Merci. I would appreciate it."

Once he left, the girls turned on her. "What did you do to get on his bad side?" Muffy asked. "Was that just about skipping his lunch?"

"Really, Hannah, the handyman?"

Hannah ignored Julia's evident amused disdain and addressed Muffy. "I'm not on his bad side." She moved away from the desk. "He's just. . .exhausted." And probably hungry. She should have offered to fix him a plate.

"Of course he is." Julia's tone was condescending.

"No wonder you didn't want us to visit your home, you naughty girl." With a mocking smile, Muffy shook her finger at her. "You wanted to keep the goods all to yourself."

"Not that she could." Julia laughed. "The 'goods' are obviously not interested in what Hannah has to offer."

"You're both so wrong." Annoyed with their taunts, Hannah spoke before she thought. "I could get him interested if I wanted to."

"Sure you could." Muffy giggled.

"Yes, I could." Hannah straightened her shoulders. "Actually, he and I got along quite splendidly when he first arrived. If I wanted to, I could interest him like that." She snapped her fingers.

"Care to make a wager?"

"A wager?" Uneasy, she glanced at the door, hoping her mother or another family member wouldn't appear. Or, heaven help her, if Eric should walk by. . .

"Chickening out?" Julia's smile came catty.

"No. I just. . .I don't gamble."

Julia's thin brows shot high. "Oh, we don't have to bet

money." She walked a short distance, holding her arm up and slowly shaking her finger, as if contemplating an idea. She turned to face Hannah. "That new boutique on the avenue has the most divine hats. If you can make the handyman fall for you in. . .one month's time, I'll buy you the hat of your choice. But if you can't make him love you, then you owe me a hat of my choice. Deal?"

Hannah winced. Julia's choices were crème de la crème, the most expensive the boutiques had to offer.

"What about me?" Muffy complained. "I want in on this, too."

"Fine." Julia smiled as if she had the upper hand. "You win, you get two hats. You lose, you owe us both one."

Hannah stared at the floor, brooding over her predicament. If she still lived with her great-uncle, such a wager wouldn't have presented a problem. Uncle Bernard always gave her whatever she asked. And Julia knew right where to strike, knowing Hannah's weakness for pretty hats.

"I don't know." She hedged.

"Well, if you don't believe you can hook him, that's understandable." Julia gave a superior little shake of her head. "You're still, shall we say, inexperienced when it comes to matters of how to win a man's interest. I understand your fear of failure, dear."

Hannah set her jaw like flint. "I'm not afraid to fail."

"Then we have a bet?" Julia asked silkily.

"Yes!" Her determination to protect her pride wavered when she realized what she'd done. "Only, maybe we shouldn't—"

"Hannah?"

Before she could attempt to extricate herself from this mess, she heard the taps of her mother's pumps in the corridor. Mother appeared at the door, her expression cooling when she saw Hannah's guests. "I didn't realize you had company."

"They came to discuss plans for the Founder's Day celebration."

Her mother's features calmed. "Oh. Very well, then. I'll leave you to your discussion."

"No need, Mrs. Thomas," Julia said quickly. "We were just leaving."

"We were?" Muffy stared, at a loss.

"Yes." Julia grabbed Muffy's arm, drawing her to the door. She glanced back at Hannah. "Remember—one month. We'll be in touch." Julia left. Muffy gave a little wave and followed.

"One month?"

"Oh, it's nothing. Just a silly idea of Julia's." Hannah's face burned. Relieved her mother hadn't entered earlier and heard the challenge, she gathered the loose pages of her play and tapped them on one end, more to look busy than for any real need to have them straightened.

Her mother looked as if she might speak but instead gave a tight little nod and smile, then left the room. Hannah let the papers drop back to the desk, her eyes falling closed as her shoulders slumped in dismay.

What had she done?

If she lost, she could never afford the hats and Julia would spread her failure far and wide. She had *no choice* but to win. Somehow, before the month was out, she had to make Eric Fontaine Jr. fall madly in love with her.

❧

Rather than retire to his room after dinner, Eric decided to check out the library. Relaxing with a good book would be a pleasurable end to an exhausting day.

He stood before five shelves spread across one entire wall, surprised to see such a vast array of reading material. Tolstoy, Keats, Alcott—the list went on.

Curious to see a novel he'd heard about, he pulled a thick volume from the shelf. The subject dealt with the Civil War; the characters of the book, plantation owners of the Deep South.

A light step at the door announced he had company. He

looked up as Hannah breezed in. His heart gave a funny little jolt as it did every time he came across the spoiled young beauty. She had an appealing, unique quality about her— inherited from her exotic mother, no doubt—that blended with a classic refinement suggesting years of privileged breeding.

"Hello." She smiled in approach. Clearly she was happy to see him.

He gave a stiff, unwelcoming nod, looking back at the book in his hands. As he had done so often when she came near, he recalled her father's warning that Eric was to have nothing to do with his daughters. Eric's father had cautioned him not to do anything that would stir the pot of Eric Sr.'s past crimes, since Eric's presence there would serve as a continual reminder. "Be on your best behavior," he had told Eric. "Do nothing that would cause them a moment's grief to have you in their home."

Eric had solemnly agreed, not realizing the true extent of Father's words until he'd arrived at the Thomas residence. To ignore Hannah seemed the wisest course. Unfortunately, she was having none of it.

"What's that you have?" An intoxicating aroma of sweet flowers rushed toward him as she came close and looked over his shoulder. "Ooo—Margaret Mitchell's classic. How I would've loved to have been in that audience in California earlier this month when David O. Selznick released his preview at that charming little theater! I heard they locked the doors and told the patrons only that another movie would air in place of the one they'd come to see. Once her name rolled across the screen, the people yelled and stood up on their seats, and when the title came on, the crowd was thunderous."

He lifted his brows at her eager recounting of the story.

"I hope it comes to our theater. To have a novel made into a screenplay and received in such a delightful manner is a dream of mine, now that I've contented myself to write the stories I'll never act in. Papa wouldn't let Uncle send me to Hollywood, though I begged him to change his mind. He said I was too young, but really, it's best to start young, don't you agree?"

"I wouldn't know." Eric moved to replace the book on the shelf, and she put her hand to his sleeve. At the unexpected contact, he froze then looked at her.

"Please feel free to read it. I don't mind. If the film is released here soon, we could then compare notes on the novel versus the movie. Who's your favorite motion picture star?" She moved into her question without taking a breath, her manner making him feel a little breathless himself. "Mine is Bette Davis, though I also like Myrna Loy and Claudette Colbert. I find their acting extraordinary, don't you?"

"I've never seen them."

"Never seen them?" Her hand fell from his sleeve, and she blinked her doelike eyes, her painted mouth agape as if he'd committed a cardinal sin. "They are only the crème de la crème of the motion picture industry!"

"I've been to one movie in my life, when I was a boy, before the talkies became popular."

Her mouth dropped a little wider before she closed it and smiled. "You almost had me convinced. You naughty boy for teasing me."

That was twice in one day he'd been addressed by the title, and he didn't like it.

"If you'll excuse me, I'm heading up to my room."

Before he could leave, she grabbed his sleeve again. "Oh, please don't go! I'll simply *expire* from boredom if you don't stay and talk. Or perhaps we might listen to the radio?" The last she offered hopefully, again dropping her hand from his sleeve, slowly this time as if embarrassed.

He looked at her shining face and glowing eyes. She looked far from expiring.

"I have another long day ahead. I should get some sleep."

"But—it's hardly gone past nine o'clock!"

"Exactly. I prefer getting to bed by ten so I can rise before dawn."

She blinked at him as if he spoke an unfamiliar language.

He managed a polite smile. "Good night, mademoiselle. Pleasant dreams."

Eric barely heard her soft good night in return.

Once he closed himself off in his room, he realized he still held her book. He didn't dare return to the library with her there and decided he may as well give it a shot and read a chapter or two before retiring.

ə

Distressed with her failed attempt at what she had hoped would be a splendid evening with Eric at her beck and call, Hannah paced the library. She could scarcely believe he'd been to only one motion picture in his entire life—surely he had been joking. She stared at the ceiling and wondered if his explanation for an early night had also been delivered in jest. He lived in New York, for pity's sake! The home of Broadway and Times Square. She had never been there, but she'd heard all about the city's glamour from Julia and Muffy, both of them frequent visitors to the Big Apple and its plethora of nightclubs.

She thought about the matchbook Eric had pulled from his pocket. Surely he had visited one or two of those places. Hannah doubted his excuse for ownership of the matches had been valid. And yet. . .he was rather an odd duck in his way of thinking.

In bed before ten?

She decided to ask him about the nightlife at her next opportunity and wondered when that might be. Certainly not tomorrow, since she'd promised to help her mother catalog items for the Ladies' Bazaar. She smiled fondly when she recalled the first of her mother's charities for which she'd volunteered. At the time, her best friend, Clemmie, had been reunited with the love of her life, a man she'd adored since childhood, the dashing Joel. Now they were happily married and living a few miles away, with a little girl on whom they both doted.

Hannah crossed her arms over her chest, hugging herself. Once she had written and sold her best-selling novel and was rolling in the dough from the profits, with her perfect house and devoted servants, she wished for what her dear friend had found. She would be eighteen soon and anticipated finding her own Romeo to her Juliet in the future. No, wait. . . that story ended in tragedy. . .a Rhett to her Scarlett, then.

She frowned, thinking of her book that their guest had taken with him to his room.

That novel also ended without Scarlett gaining her man, not even desiring his love until it was too late. Hannah enjoyed fictional drama but didn't wish to live out their tragic stories—though not all were so heartrending, only the more memorable ones.

With her head drifting in the clouds of imaginary lore, she took the staircase to her room. Once she reached the top landing, her father called out, "Who's there?"

Breaking from her trance, Hannah moved to his doorway. "It's me, Daddy." She whisked a tear from her eye before he could see.

"Kitten. . ." He called her by the pet name he used, then frowned. "Are you crying?"

"It's nothing." He would never understand her sorrow over a tale of fiction.

"Did that Fontaine character have anything to do with your tears?"

At her father's low, stern words, she blinked in confusion. "Eric?" At her familiar use of his name, her father's brows drew farther downward. "No, of course not. I was only thinking of a movie I'd seen."

He sighed and settled back, calm again. "You need to pull

your head out of those dream clouds you walk in and learn to live in the real world, Hannah."

"Yes, Daddy." She'd heard his speech a hundred times, if not more. "But if I want to be a novel writer, since I can't be an actress, I have to delve in a bit of fantasy, don't I?"

"Still nursing foolish dreams?"

She frowned. "They're not foolish. Once upon a time, women had to use a man's pseudonym for their books to be published and well received, but those days are long past. Margaret Mitchell proved that with her best seller! And others besides her."

"All right, all right. . ." He lifted his hands in a placating manner. "I know when I'm sunk. But books and movies aren't what I wanted to talk to you about."

While he spoke, her defensiveness gave way to relief, then nervousness. "Oh?"

"While our. . .houseguest is staying here, I want you to keep out of his way. He's not the kind of man I want my daughters consorting with."

That puzzled her. Of all the young men she'd known, Eric seemed the least dangerous. One certainly couldn't accuse him of a life spent in dissipation—he'd probably only had acquaintance with the word when browsing through a dictionary. And she knew his economic status didn't matter— her parents had conceived this plan of moving into the rickety old farmhouse to take their children *away* from associating with the privileged class.

"I don't understand, Daddy." She voiced her confusion. "He seems like a nice man."

"Don't let appearances deceive you, Hannah. I don't trust him, and you'd be wise to follow my lead."

Hannah could barely believe what she was hearing. Eric had done nothing to merit disfavor. He'd done his utmost to seclude himself in his room, away from the family, at every opportunity. Hadn't her parents endlessly told her not to judge people for others' mistakes and to give second chances? Her father hadn't known she'd eavesdropped on his conversation with her mother, but Hannah realized that's exactly what he was doing—judging Eric Jr. for Eric Sr.'s crimes.

The thought made her feel defensive for Eric and upset with her father. "It hardly seems fair to judge him so harshly since he's done nothing wrong."

"Han–*nah*," he stressed, "I don't want you getting involved with the man."

Involved? No, not that. The challenge to hook Eric's interest was just a challenge. If she surrendered now, the girls would spread it all over town that poor little Hannah couldn't gain the interest of the handyman. She would be whispered about and laughed at wherever she went. Once she won the bet, she would come up with a plausible excuse of why it would be best not to spend time with Eric any longer, perhaps using her father's own rule that she avoid him.

But she had no interest in getting involved with the man. He must be dull as dishwater, to retire so early and rise at dawn and have no knowledge of the entertainment industry.

She sighed. "All right, I'll be careful, Daddy. If there's nothing else, I'm going to bed."

"Good night then. I love you, Hannah. That's why I care."

Her heart warmed at his tender words, and she moved forward to kiss his cheek before retiring. She couldn't help glancing toward the opposite end of the corridor, where Eric's door stood closed.

As she prepared for bed, Hannah considered her plan. She wasn't really going against her father's wishes since she wasn't truly getting involved. Yet she didn't understand why her parents were so strict; after all, she was no longer a child.

Mother was barely seventeen when she'd married Daddy, and Clemmie a couple of weeks shy of eighteen when she married Joel. Hannah had no desire to marry anyone anytime soon, but why couldn't her parents trust her to make her own choices as they had? Besides, her little plan wouldn't hurt anyone; she would make sure of that.

Her father was so wrong about Eric. He just couldn't see it right now. But all would work out well in the end. Daddy would laugh away his groundless fears, Eric would profess his undying love, after which she would let him down easy so that perhaps they might remain friends, and she would become the proud owner of two adorable new hats from the snazziest boutique the town had to offer.

Long into the night, she mulled over Operation Hook Eric. He had barely shown her any attention the few times she had tried. Grimly, she realized if she were to succeed, she would have to resort to the most desperate of measures.

five

His third day at the Thomas residence, Eric rose before dawn, read his morning devotions, groomed, dressed, and went downstairs. A light rain tapped against the kitchen window when he greeted Mrs. Thomas as he did every morning. She always gave him breakfast, after which they drank a cup of coffee and engaged in pleasant conversation.

"I obviously won't be working on the roof today." He took a seat at the table. "I had hoped to have it finished by the end of this week. I was able to make some patches, so the leaks should be fixed over the bedrooms."

She turned from buttering toast. "Thank you! It will be so nice not to worry about these rains that come and the leaks with them." She set a plate of eggs, bacon, and toast before him.

"Merci."

"My pleasure." She retrieved their cups of coffee and took the chair across from him. "What do you feel should be the next order of business?"

"Working on the parlor walls. It gets so cold in there. My expertise extends only to patching up cracks, like with the roof. You'll want to hire professionals to replace both in the spring."

"At present, patching up is all we can manage, and we're very grateful for whatever help you can give. . . ." Her words trailed off as she looked beyond him, her expression surprised. "Hannah? Are you feeling all right, dear?"

"Of course, Mother."

At the hoarse words, Eric cast a glance over his shoulder. Hannah stood in the doorway, *stood* being a relative term since she leaned against the lintel as if it were the sole thing supporting her from sinking to the tiles. Her hair didn't look as well combed as usual, and the skin beneath her eyes appeared slightly puffy. Yet such minor flaws did nothing to detract from her rare beauty, and Eric turned back to his meal, ill at ease.

Esther scampered into the kitchen, holding a strap that buckled her schoolbooks together. She stared at Hannah. "Hello. You're up early. Are you going into New York with Muffy and Julia?"

"What's this?" Mrs. Thomas retorted sharply. "Hannah, I'll not have you go to such a city, and certainly not with those girls!"

"I'm not, Mother, I'm—"

David clomped into the kitchen, casting a curious glance at his oldest sister. "Great balls of fire! What are you doing up so early?"

"Can't a girl rise with the sun without getting the third degree?" Hannah snapped miserably.

"It's just that you've never done so before, dear." A hint of amusement touched her mother's voice.

"Why bother?" David complained. "If I didn't have to get up so darn early to walk to school, I'd sure be sleeping now."

"David, watch your language," their mother reproved.

The boy grumbled something that resembled an apology. "Wish we still lived at Uncle's and had his chauffeur to drive us."

"Eat your eggs, and be thankful for what you do have." His mother set a plate in front of him. "Many children don't have breakfast. Or nice clothes. Or a roof over their heads."

"A leaky roof," the boy complained.

"Not anymore, thanks to Mr. Fontaine." She directed a grateful smile his way.

"Humph." The boy grouched. "I'd trade it all in for a few more hours of sleep."

Mrs. Thomas sighed. Hannah moved toward the stove, poured herself a cup of coffee, and selected a piece of toast.

She brought her items to the table, taking the empty chair beside Eric. He looked back to his food before she could notice him staring.

The meal passed in relative silence.

"I need a pencil for school, Mama," Esther suddenly announced.

"What happened to the one I gave you?"

"I must have lost it on the walk home yesterday."

Her mother sighed. "You need to be more careful with your things, Esther. Very well, come with me, and I'll see if I can locate another one in the library."

"And I need more paper." David jumped up from his chair to follow.

"You wouldn't if you didn't use what I gave you on spit wads. Don't think I don't know what you've been doing, young man. . . ."

"Hard to believe they were once model children, isn't it?"

Hannah's question to Eric broke the silence that settled around them once the others left.

"They're not that much different from my brothers and sisters." Eric glanced her way—into huge, light-colored eyes, noting how soft the thick fringes of her long black lashes were—which suddenly made him realize how close she'd scooted to him.

He stood and grabbed his plate, taking it to the sink.

"You're not leaving?" she asked, clearly unhappy with the idea.

"I have work to do."

"But you haven't finished your coffee."

Eric glanced at his half-filled cup, wanting both the warmth and the boost before entering the cold parlor. "I'll take it with me." He picked it up by its saucer and left.

Inside the parlor, he took sips of the hot brew as he walked around the room, studying its walls and figuring out his next course of action. He'd told Mrs. Thomas he would need to rip away the paper to make repairs, which meant the walls would be an eyesore, but she'd assured him that the room's temperature was more important than dingy displays of cabbage roses and that she hoped to repaper the walls in any case.

He had pulled the furniture away from the baseboards when a footfall from behind captured his attention. He looked over his shoulder.

Hannah entered the room.

&

"Please, don't let me disturb you." Hannah smiled and moved toward the desk he'd pulled away from the wall. She laid down her notebook and sat down, noting he still stared as if uncertain why she'd come.

Simpering in the same way Muffy did hadn't gained her an ounce of coveted attention or the kind smile he'd given her friend. She wasn't so bold as to come on to him like gangbusters as Julia had done, either, so she needed to devise her own schemes.

"I work best in this room because it has the most windows for light," she explained, opening the notebook she'd unearthed from its hiding place in the library. "The ladies' committee has commissioned me to write a play for the Founder's Day picnic." Though she received no pay for her volunteer work, she hoped her words sounded important enough to impress him.

He gave a little grunt and turned back to study the wall. "I can start in another room so I won't bother you."

"No! I mean, you won't bother me." She could also move to another room, but that would defeat her purpose in being here—to put herself wherever he was so he couldn't help but notice her.

Of course, that proved difficult when his back was constantly turned her way.

Lightly tapping pen on paper, she, on the other hand,

had a clear and constant view of his fine physique as he cut sections of the old, brittle wallpaper with a knife and peeled it from the wall. She wondered if he engaged in sports to be so toned, trim, and agile, or if his work at the mission had honed him to perfection.

He turned suddenly and caught her staring.

Her face flushed hot, and she dropped her gaze to the paper where she'd written three whole words: *We will prevail.*

He moved toward the door, arresting her attention.

"Where are you going?"

At her breathless rush of words, he looked at her a little strangely. "To the shed. I'm hoping your father has a bag of plaster to caulk up the cracks and provide temporary insulation."

She shrugged, relieved that he was coming back. "I'm not sure what's out there, but he purchased a number of items he would need before he had his accident."

Eric nodded and left the parlor.

Hannah sighed, dropped her pen, and gracefully slumped back in the chair. Perhaps the colonists in her play had prevailed, but she wasn't doing so well.

This would take more thought. If she were bold like Julia, she would unbutton the top two buttons of her blouse and sit so as to bring attention to her shapely legs. If she were gregarious like Muffy, she might continuously clear her throat or make little humming noises now and then to remind Eric of her presence. But she was no seductress, and she certainly didn't want to come across as annoying. Since planting herself against the wall in his line of vision was clearly out of the question, she would have to resort to a different method.

A possibility came to mind that held no appeal. However, she didn't see how it could fail and dourly resigned herself to initiate a new phase to her plan.

❧

With the items he needed located and prepared, Eric drew out his time in the shed until he felt sure Hannah would have given up and left the parlor. Upon his return, he realized his mistake.

"I was beginning to think we might need to send a search party after you." Hard at work with whatever she wrote, Hannah looked over her shoulder and greeted him with a bright smile, dimples flashing in her cheeks. "Oh my. How'd you get so wet?"

"It is raining." Struck anew by her beauty, he attempted a return smile and moved back to the wall. He used a piece of sheeting to rub most of the dampness from his clothes, keeping his back to her. At least that way he could almost forget her existence in the room; whatever perfume she wore filled the air with the scent of flowers. He tossed down his makeshift towel and set to work.

When he heard the chair skid back and her footfall, followed by a stronger wash of those flowers, his hand tightened on the mixing stick.

She dropped to her knees close beside him. He turned a startled glance her way.

"Hannah?" Her mother's voice preceded her as she approached the door.

Eric jumped up so fast he almost knocked over the pail of plaster paste.

Dressed in a slicker, Mrs. Thomas lifted her brow but thankfully didn't address the issue of why they'd been kneeling so close to one another. He didn't want her mother getting the wrong idea.

"The rain is coming down harder. I'll need to run the children to school. I don't want them coming down with what Abbie has."

"Mother, are you sure?"

Eric detected worry in Hannah's voice and glanced at her as she slowly rose to her feet.

"You know Daddy won't like it."

Mrs. Thomas smiled. "I'll be fine as long as there are no

sudden stops. It's only a couple of miles."

She disappeared, and Hannah grabbed Eric's sleeve. He had the impression she didn't even realize she'd done so. "Daddy doesn't like her driving in bad weather; she's not good at the wheel. She gets very nervous in thunderstorms."

He nodded and hurried after her mother. "Mrs. Thomas!" He caught her just walking out the door. "Why not let me drive them? I need to drop by the drugstore and pick up a few things I forgot. This would give me the opportunity."

"But you don't know your way around town."

"I'll go along too," Hannah offered quickly.

"Well, I don't know. . . ."

"I'm a good driver," Eric assured. "I often use the family car to run errands for the mission."

"And if you're gone when Daddy wakes up," Hannah added, "he won't like it."

"You're right about that. Very well. Thank you." Mrs. Thomas handed Eric the keys. "Children, hurry. You don't want to be late."

David and Esther appeared in yellow slickers and matching bonnets. "Do we have to go? Can't we stay home since it's raining?" David groused.

"Of course not."

Hannah rummaged through the coats in the front closet and retrieved a black slicker.

"Have you no raincoat?" she asked Eric.

"I'll be fine."

"You'll be soaked in this deluge, and we wouldn't want you to catch a cold, either. Here. It's Josiah's. He left it behind."

He nodded his thanks and shrugged into the borrowed raincoat while she did the same with a smaller version in a navy color. He grabbed his hat, and she pulled a rain bonnet over her disheveled hair, then led him to a Packard beside the house. Eric pulled up the collar of the slicker, hunching his shoulders against the rain. The children ran behind and jumped in the car. Eric opened Hannah's door, waiting for her to get inside and shutting it before hurrying to duck in behind the wheel.

Visibility was poor, the flashes of lightning in the distance filling the skies and causing Esther to squeal each time. Eric drove carefully along the country road and across a covered bridge, the stream below frothing in its mad rush along the rocks.

Soon Hannah told him to make a right turn, which took them into the business district of the small community. At the schoolhouse, they dropped off the children, and Hannah instructed him how to find the drugstore. Once there, he ran inside, ducking the storm as best he could, and bought a box of baking soda to brush his teeth and extra shaving supplies. He had no idea how long he would be staying at the Thomas residence, but with the miserable shape of the house and the uncooperative weather, it could be awhile.

On the drive back, the storm began to diminish, enough to be heard without practically shouting over the rain, and Hannah took the opportunity. "Does New York get much bad weather?"

"We live beside the Atlantic Ocean." He grinned, casting her a sidelong glance. "What do you think?"

"I've never been to the ocean, never been much of anywhere, though we did live upstate when I was a child—in a children's reformatory on a farm. My father worked there, helping to keep things in repair, and my uncle was—still is—the schoolmaster."

"At the Lyons farm?" he asked in surprise.

"You know them?"

"My father didn't name names in public, of course, but he told my family. The Lyonses came to see him years ago."

"Yes, I remember that day; I was six." Her voice sounded tight. "My father went to see him with Uncle Stewart and Aunt Charleigh—they're not really my aunt and uncle by blood, but I call them that because our families are close.

Lady Annabelle's son and his fiancé were staying at the farm. They were running from a gangster and seeking refuge. That's how they found out about your father living close by."

"Really?" His brows went up.

"Yes, I overheard them talking one night. So tell me, what's it like in New York City? It must be wonderful on Broadway, with the glamour and lights. Both Julia and Muffy have said it's spectacular. Of course, I know that live entertainment is different from motion pictures, but it's still entertainment, isn't it? I once aspired to be an actress, but Mama wouldn't allow the lessons." She scarcely took a breath. "Oh dear. I'm doing it again, aren't I? I have a tendency to ramble in conversation."

"No, it's fine." Her mix of breathless sentences hadn't annoyed him. At least now she acted more like herself and less like her friends: gushing in the library the previous evening and being so bold that morning.

"But you still haven't told me. What's Broadway like?" She twisted to sit sideways for a better look at him. "I'd like to hear a man's perspective."

"I've never been."

"What?"

He didn't miss the profound shock in her voice. "I thought you lived close to the city."

"We do."

"But. . ." She shook her head as if unable to fathom the idea. "How can you live there all your life and never visit Broadway? I know you've been to the nightclubs. I saw your matchbook."

"Like I told your mother, it wasn't mine."

She gaped at him. "You're serious."

"Not everyone who lives in New York takes part in the nightlife."

"But you live so close! It just seems odd that you would never have visited."

"Mother warned all of us, as far back as I can remember,

never to go there. Father agreed."

"But I thought he—" She ended her words abruptly, but he understood what she didn't say.

"Prowled the city, engaging in all the depravity it had to offer? He did at one point. Before he met Mother. The gangsters he'd been involved with who live there still pose a threat, another reason my parents warned us not to go there. My father really has changed."

"I believe you." Her tone came soft, barely heard above the patter of rain.

He glanced her way, for the first time relaxing. "Thank you for that. Still, I'm certain your parents—your father especially—will be relieved once I'm gone. My father and your father had quite an illustrious association with those gangsters."

"My father? Oh, you mean how he got involved with those men. Owing them money for a loan, I imagine."

"I don't know about that." He shook his head. "I meant when they worked together for Vittorio Piccoli."

"My father worked for the Piccoli mob?"

"You didn't know?"

"I—I knew some—"

At her stunned behavior, he winced, realizing too late he shouldn't have spoken. His father had never withheld one sordid act he'd done, sharing his testimony with the suffering as a means of offering hope that God could forgive them, too. It hadn't crossed Eric's mind that Hannah wouldn't know about her father's past.

With relief, he noticed the farmhouse come into view and pulled into the drive. He walked around and opened the door for Hannah. She didn't move, staring straight ahead.

"Are you all right?"

His quiet words snapped her out of whatever trance held her spellbound, and she accepted his help from the car. "Thank you."

He nodded and walked with her into the house. Once he

put away his borrowed rain gear, he returned to the parlor and resumed his task. Not to his surprise, Hannah came in behind him.

He heard the chair slide away as she took a seat behind the desk. After a short time, the chair again skidded on the floor, and he heard her approach. He didn't look her way until she sank to her knees beside him, as she'd done before. This time, she didn't do it boldly, as if she might pounce, but seemed insecure, her palms touching each other, clasped between her legs in the folds of her skirt.

"Can I help?"

His mouth parted in shock. "You want to help me?"

"I find it difficult to concentrate on my play."

"I'm sorry." He felt bad. "I shouldn't have told you like that."

"It's all right." She smiled faintly. "I'm glad at least someone in this house is honest with me."

He winced, hearing a hint of underlying anger in her tone. "Don't be upset with your father. He must have had good reason for not telling you."

"Hmm." She averted her attention to the pail. "Show me how it's done?"

"No, really, I can handle it. You don't have to—"

"I want to. I'm bored, and it might be fun."

Fun? "I only have one stick."

"I can remedy that." Before he could stop her, she broke it in half. "Now we have two."

At the bright smile she gave, her bleak mood lifting, he managed to curb a groan.

"Oui, it seems we do." The shorter stick would make it harder to dip into the paste without submerging his fingers, but he didn't really want to wade back through the storm to the shed to find another.

He made one, last-ditch effort. "You might end up ruining that pretty dress."

His warning had the opposite effect as her expression softened. "You think my dress is pretty?"

He did, but not half as pretty as the girl wearing it. At the sudden thought, he looked away from her shimmering eyes and focused on his task, dipping the decapitated stick into the goo and smearing it over a crack. "It's all right, as ladies' dresses go. Point is, you'll get it dirty, and it looks as if it cost a small fortune."

"Yes, that's true." She looked uncertain; then her face brightened again. "I'll be right back. Don't go anywhere!"

Before he could respond, she jumped up and dashed out of the parlor.

six

Hannah sorted through the box of charity items her mother had collected for the next bazaar, recalling she'd thrown in some of Josiah's ill-fitting clothes. Finding a pair of denim jeans and a flannel shirt, she held them up to her. Baggy, but a sash belt would hold them up, and she could roll up the sleeves.

Excited that the first step of her plan was working, she ducked into her room to change.

Rising at dawn had been a challenge; every muscle in her young body had complained at leaving her soft warm bed. A dusting of powder had done little to eliminate signs of weariness beneath her eyes, and her hair had frizzed due to the humidity. The pretty blue dress and coat of lipstick had helped, but she'd been tempted to crawl back into bed and forget the whole thing. A glance at one of her hats had brutally reminded her of the challenge and acted as the push to send her out the door.

Now, she tied her thick hair back with a ribbon, the thought of combing out plaster bits not appealing. She glanced in the mirror, wincing at the thought of Julia and Muffy dropping by unannounced and catching her in such drab clothes, and men's clothes at that! But sometimes sacrifice was imperative to achieve success.

Her door opened as she knotted the silk sash around her waist. She watched in the mirror as her mother entered, her arms full of folded linens. Her eyes widened in surprise to see Hannah's attire. She turned to face her mother, bolstering her courage.

"I've decided to help Eric—that is, Mr. Fontaine—with the repairs."

"Really?" Her mother drew out the word softly. She looked at Hannah a moment before moving to the bureau and opening the top drawer, tucking several items inside. "May I ask what brought about this sudden decision?"

In the face of her mother's seeming calm, Hannah floundered for an answer. "If he has help, it will mean we'll have a warm house much sooner, if not a better one. Though I still don't see why we had to leave Uncle's in the first place."

"Your father and I have our reasons."

A twinge of resentment made her blurt, "Just like you had your reasons for keeping it secret about Daddy being a gangster?" Her mother swung around, her lips parting in dread surprise and confirming Eric's words. "Yes, Mother, I know. Why did you never tell me?"

"Did Mr. Fontaine tell you this?"

"It slipped out in conversation. He had the mistaken impression that our family is truthful with one another."

Her mother sighed. "We thought it best to leave such details in the past, where they belong. They no longer concern our family."

"Don't they?" Hannah spread her hands in confusion. "How can Daddy hate Eric's father so much, if he was also a criminal?"

"It's complicated, Hannah. And he doesn't hate him, not really."

She shook her head. "I just don't understand how he can be so, so hypocritical."

"Hannah! Do not say such things about your father."

"You both taught me never to play judge and jury. What happened to giving second chances, Mother? To honesty?"

She closed her eyes on another sigh. "We felt it best to shield our children from the crimes your father once committed. We wanted. . .a fresh start."

"So why won't Daddy give Mr. Fontaine a chance for a fresh start?"

"I cannot speak for your father. But in all he does, in every decision he makes, he does so for the protection of our family."

Hannah knew that to be true, knew that he loved them, but still couldn't help feeling betrayed as well as upset over the critical words he'd spoken about Eric.

"I've had several occasions to speak with our guest," her mother continued, "and I find him to be a pleasant young man raised on good, solid principles. It may take longer for your father to see, but a person's true character always does come out."

"I hope so." A smattering of guilt made Hannah fidget and study the cracks in the floor. "Daddy warned me from spending time alone with him. But I don't understand why. He's very nice."

Regardless of her plan to hook him, Hannah had seen his kindness and felt another rush of remorse for having agreed to Julia's challenge. If her mother learned of Hannah's true reason for wanting to spend time in Eric's company, she would be ashamed of her daughter.

"I will speak with your father."

Hannah looked up sharply. "Then you don't mind if I help Eric?"

Her mother regarded her in surprise. "My feelings would matter to you?"

"Of course." Hannah felt bad for the words she'd earlier spouted. "I care about your opinion."

Her mother's rigid expression eased into relief. "Then I will tell you, my dear. You may think you're a woman, and in many ways you are, but all too often you think as a child. So I give you this advice, Hannah: Be as wise as a serpent and as harmless as a dove. Do nothing that one day you may have cause to regret."

Those words haunted Hannah as she returned downstairs. Could Mother somehow know of the challenge? No, it wasn't possible. If her mother had guessed, her words to Hannah wouldn't have been so civil.

She stepped into the parlor, and Eric looked over his shoulder. His eyes widened in clear shock at her appearance, but she trusted that with the pretty sash and hair ribbon and the dab of fresh lipstick she didn't look too bad.

"Here I am," she said needlessly.

"I've been thinking. Maybe you shouldn't help with this. I don't think your father would approve of your being in my company more than necessity allows."

She bristled at that. Did everyone think her such a child? "I've just spoken with Mother, and she approved, so there's no longer a problem." She approached and knelt back down, picking up the stick. "Just show me what to do."

Eric's attitude grudging, he did as she asked. As the morning passed into afternoon, she tried to initiate conversation, but he'd gone into a brooding silence, and she realized that whatever the reason, *he* had a problem with her being there.

She withheld a sigh. It would take patience and time, but eventually she would win him over.

ಶ

Eric couldn't figure Hannah out. When they met, she had seemed reserved and anxious, which made sense, given the circumstances. After the last visit from her socialite friends, for some curious reason she'd tried to imitate their annoying traits. But when she appeared in unfashionable men's work clothes, which made her look home-girl cute and not at all boyish, ready to help, as she'd done every day this week, he'd been entirely flummoxed.

Just what was her game?

He had relented, hoping the two of them working together could speed the process up and he'd be out of everyone's way that much faster. Though "help" could hardly describe her actions, and instead of speeding things up, she'd slowed them down.

He wondered why he even put up with her shoddy attempts, her ignorance in the most basic of tasks not coming as a surprise due to her former privileged life. He felt sorry for the spoiled little princess, even befriended her, though he hoped he hadn't made a mistake in doing that.

Today they'd spackled the last wall in the parlor. Already he could tell a difference in the room's temperature and no longer felt as if he walked inside a refrigerated box. Splotches of hardened gray plaster covered damaged spots where paper had been torn away. He wondered if he would be asked to help with the wallpapering, then decided he should offer since his repairs had been responsible for making the walls a monstrosity.

The family hardly seemed impoverished, at least in matters of money; they certainly didn't suffer like those who visited the mission. But Eric reasoned that Mr. Thomas had little to no money left, after buying the property, to hire professional help. The house was huge, with six bedrooms and three baths, and who knew how many more rooms? He hadn't counted and had no idea how long it would take to go through each and accomplish any necessary repairs. With Hannah's sloppy work and his need to redo her mistakes, additional cleanup amounted to hours. He wondered if he would be out of here by Christmas.

Still, as he told himself numerous times a day, it was for a good cause. This family needed his help, though he sensed the eldest daughter needed a far different kind of help, help he wasn't sure he knew how to give.

What made him think of her?

And where could she be?

She had told him she would return soon. That had been at least a quarter of an hour ago. Likely she was again working on her little play or fantasizing over some movie, playing it out in her mind, her head, as usual, in the clouds. How many times had he repeated her name when she was immersed in some movie fantasy, as she'd then explained to him and in great detail?

Shaking his head to scatter thoughts of Hannah, whom he certainly did not need to think about, Eric saw he needed more plaster. He picked up the bucket and left the room to make another trip to the shed. He stopped in his tracks, across from the stairwell, stunned at the sight that met his eyes.

Hannah lay draped over the top of the newly waxed split-level banister, stomach down. As he gaped, he watched her push at the bevel post to catapult her descent. Like butter over a griddle, she flew down the narrow rail. Anxious when he saw her teeter to one side, Eric dropped the pail and rushed forward, lifting his arms to catch her.

His hands made contact with her hips, sliding to a stop at her waist before her bottom could hit the large beveled post at the main landing. She let out a startled gasp and tried to look over her shoulder, almost losing her grip on the banister and toppling to the stairs.

"Steady," Eric warned, keeping his hands fixed on her as she pulled one denim-clad leg up over the rail to meet with the other on the bottom stair.

"What were you doing?" He addressed her in stupefied disbelief the moment she faced him. Her fair skin flushed the color of a pink rose, her gaze skittering from her feet to the front door.

A burst of clapping came from above, drawing Eric's attention to the top landing, where Abbie leaned over the rail in excitement. "You did it, Hannah! You did it!" She ran to the railing. "Watch me! Catch me, too!"

Before Eric could bat an eyelid, Abbie came hurtling toward him. He raised his hands to catch her before she could make painful contact with the post. "I did it, I did it!" she squealed as he peeled her off the railing and set her on her feet.

He looked back and forth between sisters. Hannah now

looked at him, embarrassment in her eyes.

"Hannah used to slide down the banister at Uncle's house," Abbie explained, "but I was too scared. Mama just polished them, and Hannah said that's when they're best for sliding. I said it was too scary, and she said it wasn't so bad as it was at Uncle's 'cause they're split-level here and not so high—"

"Abbie, that's enough," Hannah reproved quietly. "I'm sure Mr. Thomas doesn't care to hear of our silly doings."

"Wait'll Esther hears. She always calls me a baby. Just wait'll she hears." With that, Abbie ran from the foyer, leaving the two of them alone.

"Um, thanks for catching me. I'd forgotten how slick those rails could be."

Eric nodded and retraced his steps to pick up the pail.

"You must think me rather foolish." She followed him. "The children miss the other place, and I had hoped to cheer Abbie."

"You don't owe me any explanations." Eric studied her. "Though it does seem that you take having fun a little too seriously."

Her eyes were curious. "I'm not sure I understand."

"I've been here over a week and have noticed, if you're not lost in some fantasy, all you can think about is the next good time to be had. You take the idea to a new extreme. I'm not sure why you offered to help me, because you even try making a game out of that."

She frowned. "And what's so wrong with operating on the bright side of things? As long as the job gets done."

"Do you ever notice a darker side exists?"

She shook her head in confusion. "Why should I try?"

"Because there's more to life than silly parties and fantasy stories."

She gaped at him in clear shock. "I'm not sure why you would say that to me. When have I talked about parties? Okay, yes, I did ask about the nightlife in New York City—is that what you mean? But writing the play is my life right now. Is that so wrong? Besides, I do other things. I've helped Mother with cataloging her bazaars. And that can be awfully tedious work. And I've helped you this past week, haven't I? I'm not entirely helpless, as you seem to think."

He refrained from telling her he could have finished three rooms alone in the time it took to do one with her help, keeping in mind her inexperience and not wanting to hurt her feelings after hearing her impassioned speech.

"I never said you're helpless. It's not that I'm ungrateful. I realize you're trying to help." He shook his head as he struggled with what should be said and what should remain silent. "Let's just drop it, all right?" He moved to the door and opened it, walking across the grounds to the shed. He heard her footsteps rustle in the leaves behind him.

"No, let's not drop it. I want to know what you meant."

He turned, and she backed up a quick step. He hadn't realized how close to his heels she'd been. "You really want to know?"

"I said so, didn't I?"

"You have no concept of the real world."

She laughed. "That's absurd. Of course I do."

"Do you?" He waved a hand toward the house in back of her. "You turn your cute little nose up at the house your father bought your family"—he realized the terminology he'd used to describe her nose and hurried ahead, hoping she didn't catch his slip—"and I couldn't begin to count how many families would consider this place a godsend and be grateful for such a roof over their heads, even with all its flaws."

She blinked and he wondered what she was thinking. "It's just beneath what we're used to."

"Yes, I know. Your great-uncle's vast mansion. Tell me, do you even know that this country has been suffering a major depression for the past ten years?"

"Of course. I haven't been living in a cave."

"Haven't you? You concentrate on such foolish nonsense when there are more worthwhile endeavors to pursue."

"Tell me that you are not calling my play foolish nonsense! One day my works will achieve nationwide acclaim—you'll see. Then you'll have to eat those words, Eric Fontaine!"

He snorted. "Who cares about a silly play when a person's belly is cramping from starvation? When they don't have a dime to buy a meal and use boxes in the alley for a bed?"

She winced. "Not everyone can run a mission."

"Maybe not, but you don't have to turn a blind eye to the suffering of a nation."

She threw her hands up to shoulder level. "What do you want me to do about it? I'm just one person."

"If everyone had that attitude, our country would have gone to the dogs a long time ago. It takes only one person to make a difference, Hannah. Instead of focusing on all the recent motion picture releases and the stars who make them, try looking at the actual world around you for a change. Life isn't composed of a celluloid movie. Those stories and characters aren't even real!"

She tilted her chin up defensively. "My Aunt Darcy taught me there should be a balance in life. That a person shouldn't spend all their time working but should have fun, too. 'All work and no play makes Jack a dull boy'—isn't that how the saying goes? She made even work fun—holding fence-painting contests with her pies as a prize, and the like. Your problem is the same as my uncle's was: You think everything has to be work, work, work."

"It seems to me, since he owns a mansion and spends most of his time globetrotting, he's an A-1 candidate for a good time."

"Wrong uncle. I'm talking about Uncle Brent and Aunt Darcy, who live at Lyons Refuge—the children's reformatory farm I told you about. Uncle Brent didn't know how to have fun, either, until Aunt Darcy came along." A smug expression tilted her mouth. "Besides, I heard that since Europe made requests for weaponry due to the war with Hitler raging over there, Connecticut has opened jobs at the munitions factories to many people in our state who were out of work."

His surprise at her knowledge of the affairs of her state, much less that there was a war going on, must have shown, because she scowled at him and lifted her chin higher. "I'm not a dunce. I do hear about current affairs."

"Hearing about them isn't the same as experiencing them firsthand."

"So, let me get this straight: You think I should sleep in a box or go without a meal to experience what the unfortunate in our country are suffering."

"I think you should open your eyes to the real world and stop living with your head in the clouds."

"And I think you should learn that a little fun won't kill you and can make the drudgery of a task disappear."

"I know how to have fun."

"Do you?"

Eric shook his head in exasperation, suddenly realizing they stood toe-to-toe in the middle of the yard, arguing at a level to be heard from inside the house. She smiled sweetly, alerting him to possible trouble.

"I have a proposition for you."

He narrowed his eyes. "What sort of proposition?"

"You seem to think I have no concept of the real world. I question if you know what it's like to have fun. You choose something for me to experience that will satisfy your idea of what's 'real.' But you have to agree to spend an afternoon doing something I think is fun. Agreed?" She stuck out her hand.

He glanced down at it then back into her eyes. "Your parents might not go along with that."

She frowned. "I can make my own decisions. But if it'll

make you feel better, I'll clear it with Mother first."

He put out his hand, but before she could grasp it, he pulled away. "If both your parents agree, then we have a deal."

"Of course."

He brought his hand forward and clasped hers, noticing how his large hand engulfed her small one. A rush of warmth made him swiftly pull his hand away.

"I need to get back to work on the roof."

"I thought we were finishing the wall."

He felt the need to distance himself from Hannah. "While we finally have a sunny day, I should be up on that roof, finishing repairs. I should have resumed this morning."

"All right. Let me throw a coat on. It's a bit nippy."

"What—why?" He stopped her with a hand to her sleeve then instantly dropped it away.

"To help you, of course."

"*You* are not going up on that roof."

She cast a doubtful glance upward then at the ladder he'd left leaning on the side of the house. "I could bring you what you need—"

"Non. Your parents would never forgive me if you fell."

She sighed. "All right then. I suppose I should spend time working on the play. Clear your calendar for Saturday, though, and I'll plan our outing then."

"After you talk to your mother."

"I told you I would." She pouted, and he nodded, the deal made.

She turned to go then pivoted on her heel. "Remember, this Saturday. . ."

"I won't forget."

He wished he could.

seven

Once Saturday arrived, Hannah sat in a muddle of confusion, unable to concentrate on her story. At least she'd finished the first act of the play, but she was having kittens trying to finish the next chapter of her novel. Worse, the hero rescuer had begun to develop the physical traits of a certain houseguest.

She threw down her pen. This was getting her nowhere. Maybe if she had Great-Uncle Bernard's typewriter. . . . Who was she trying to fool? The writing implement wasn't the problem. The real problem hammered up on the roof. She turned her eyes up to the ceiling and wished. . .what?

Nothing about getting involved, surely. Among other good reasons for why it would be a very bad idea: If she allowed her feelings to get in the way, they might prevent her from following through with her plan.

She didn't need two new hats but certainly couldn't afford to buy them. Where would she get the money? She supposed she could somehow find a ride to the mansion, but if her mother ever got wind that she'd asked Great-Uncle Bernard for money, Hannah would be in bigger trouble than if her mother learned she had agreed to the challenge. For some reason, lately her mother wanted nothing to do with her uncle, and that forced distance included the rest of the family, as well.

Hannah had no choice but to win.

Looking at the clock, she shrieked. Only an hour left before her outing with Eric. Pushing away from the desk, she hurried to her room. Her plan was ingenious really, similar to the agreement Aunt Darcy once made with Uncle Brent. Deciding against wearing boys' jeans, she chose a skirt that would give ample leg room but was fitted enough not to risk getting tangled in the bike gears or chain. If anyone outside her home spotted her in drab men's attire, she would be humiliated. Besides, she had to look her best if she was going to interest Eric, who still seemed to prefer being anywhere else than with her.

Tying a paisley silk scarf at her neck to match her pale yellow sweater, she nodded in approval, then pulled on her hat and coat.

After collecting a wicker basket from the kitchen, she met Eric downstairs. He appeared ill at ease, his eyes taking in certain areas of the room, as if they refused to settle on her for long.

"You still haven't told me where we're going," he greeted.

She smiled. "I thought it high time you saw more of Cedarbrook."

"We're going for a drive?"

"Even better." She crooked her finger playfully. "Come along. You won't be disappointed."

He held back, as if he might refuse, then gave a short nod and followed her outside to the shed.

"We're going to work on more home improvements?" he asked, puzzled.

"No, silly. This." She moved to the side of the shed where she'd pulled out the bike earlier, when a sudden worrisome thought struck. "You do know how to ride one of these?"

He eyed the long bicycle. "I've never ridden a two-seater."

"Oh, it's a breeze. You'll get the hang of it in no time. I'll sit here." She patted the front seat. "And you take the back." She congratulated herself on her idea. This way she would be in his line of vision the entire time, since she would need to steer, due to his inexperience.

"I'm not sure. . . ." He glanced up at the overcast skies. "It might rain."

"The sky has looked like that for days, and no rain yet.

Chicken?" she inquired sweetly. "I assumed you were the type to boldly take on new challenges, unafraid. Was I wrong?" With innocent playfulness, she batted her eyelashes.

"Lead the way," he growled with a narrow-eyed smile.

She laughed and, with some instruction to him, put her basket in the wire container at the front. They mounted their separate seats, Hannah tucking her skirt up as best she could so it wouldn't get in the way. After a wobbly start, they headed down the drive and to the empty country road.

Here the ground lay flat, though inclines and descents loomed in the distance, but she felt that together they could manage without a problem. On both sides, trees of all types loomed overhead, their branches forming a shadowed canopy. Many still bloomed in chaotic hues encompassing a bold spectrum of reds, oranges, and yellows. Some had lost their leaves, while the evergreens remained refreshing pillars of green scattered among the deciduous trees.

Despite the brisk air that blew into her face, Hannah glowed with warmth. She had finally achieved her purpose—to pull Eric away from work and spend quality time with him, ending any likelihood of one of her sisters or her mother entering the room, which had happened with annoying frequency.

They came to another road that branched off to a secluded spot she enjoyed. "We're turning here," she called over her shoulder.

Soon they pulled alongside a pond, sparkling with the noon-day sun that streamed through the top boughs of the dense thicket surrounding it. Once they dismounted, she grabbed the wicker basket and pulled out a cloth, spreading it on the ground.

He observed her with an expression of utter disbelief. "Isn't it a little cold for a picnic?"

"It's not so bad." She knelt on the cloth, the chill of the ground seeping through to her knees, and rethought her position and her words. She sat down, her coat blocking the chill. "Just long enough to eat a sandwich?"

He continued staring at her.

"What?"

"I just never figured you for the outdoor type. I thought you preferred functions that the socialites take part in."

"I enjoy dances and parties, certainly, but my father taught us an appreciation for the outdoors. This pond"—she waved a hand toward the water—"will soon be frozen. Daddy usually takes us here for ice skating. He's very much the American outdoorsman, and Mother is an island princess. Some might call their union strange, but they're perfect for one another."

"Your mother is a princess?" He lowered himself beside her, taking a seat. "You mean in the literary sense? Saying she's a wonderful lady?"

"Well, she's that, too, though I get frustrated with her views sometimes. But no, I mean royalty in the literal sense. Her father, my grandfather, is a missionary on a South Pacific island. The chief gave his daughter, my grandmother, to him as a gift, so to speak, though my grandfather didn't take advantage of that, of course. She served him, though he made her sleep in a separate hut, and they fell in love over the course of time and married. Mother was their only child who lived. My grandmother died in childbirth with their second child."

"I had no idea." Eric looked dazed. "That explains a lot."

Curious, she tilted her head while handing him a sandwich. "What?"

"Your life," he said distantly, as though his thoughts lay elsewhere. "Your ideas about it. Your mother's bearing. So your grandfather, where is he?"

"He's still on the island. I've never met him."

"And your Great-Uncle Bernard is your grandfather's brother?"

She nodded. "From what I understand, they didn't get along. My great-uncle never supported my grandfather's missionary work—or rather, him leaving the family tuna business to become one. He has nothing against giving to charities and has been known to support them."

They ate their sandwiches while looking out over the pond.

"What did you mean when you said Mother being a princess explains how I think about life?" she asked, his words niggling at her.

"I didn't mean that to sound like a bad thing. . . ."

She nodded for him to continue.

"It's just that you seem to live your life in fantasy after fantasy. Knowing your roots now and that your mother is a—" He stopped speaking and looked at her. "Wait. If she's a princess, that makes you one, too, doesn't it?"

"Yes. All of my sisters, actually."

"So it's no wonder you've lived such a pampered life."

She frowned. Did he think she was spoiled? At least she volunteered at her mother's charity functions. "Wrong side of the family. My mother's mother and my great-uncle aren't related."

"Oh right." He crumpled up the wax paper and tossed it into the basket. "It's so cold, I guess my brain froze there for a minute."

"Are you really that cold?" She wore layers, but the cold from the ground had started to seep through her coat to her backside. "We have chocolate cream pie from the bakery for dessert—"

He looked up at the sky. "Did you feel that?"

"Feel what?" She followed his glance upward. "I don't feel anything."

"Something wet just hit me. There it is again." He jumped to his feet. "It's going to rain."

"Are you sure?" She looked at the overcast sky that seemed rather bright for rain. "Maybe it's from the pond."

"There's no wind to carry water this way. It's going to rain, and we need to get back before the sky unleashes on our heads."

"All right, if you insist." She gave in with a little pout.

He helped her up, and she regretted when he pulled his hands away, even if they were as cold as hers. He grabbed the hamper and stuffed the blanket inside and then set the hamper in the wire basket.

Halfway home, the sky let loose with icy droplets. She squealed as they hit her face, and Eric called out to her, "How good are you on one of these things?"

"I have years of experience," she called back over her shoulder. "Why?"

"If we're going to make it to the house before we're drenched, we need to pedal faster. Can you do it?"

"Yes." She hadn't ridden the bicycle in months, but her legs felt almost numb, and her hands didn't feel like a part of her, either.

They increased pace. Regardless, the droplets fell faster. Seeing white, she opened her eyes wide in shock. "That's snow!"

Hoping they would make it back before the road grew slick, she hunched her shoulders and kept her head low, pedaling fast and wincing at the burn in her legs. To her relief, the old farmhouse soon loomed into view, and she steered them into the drive, her heart thumping against her ribs when she almost overshot her mark and sent them skidding into the leaves.

"We made it!" She braked at the shed. He got off quickly, but she had difficulty dismounting, her legs wobbly and barely feeling connected to her body.

"Are you all right?" He caught her in his arms as she brought her other leg over the bicycle. She fell into him, and he tightened his hold, both of them helplessly laughing. The bike fell against her. She groaned, and he moved them away from it.

"Better?" he asked.

"I don't think I'll walk ever again," she moaned. Being

held against him, even as wet as they'd gotten, felt nice, and she didn't want it to end, though she didn't exaggerate. Her thighs and calves burned like fire, and the rest of her legs felt as if they didn't belong to her.

His hand slipped around her waist as he tried to help her walk. She stumbled, and he brought his other arm up fast around her midriff as her knees buckled. He'd barely brought them both aright, when she felt him wrenched away from her.

Frantic at the sudden loss of support, she reached for a nearby tree, her eyes widening.

"Josiah?" she whispered.

"Keep your hands off my sister!" Her older brother growled the warning from between clenched teeth as he shoved Eric back against the shed and held him there by his coat lapels. "What did you do to her?"

"Josiah—stop it!" She raised her voice to be heard. "Eric didn't do anything. We were cycling hard to get out of the bad weather, and it's taking me awhile to get my balance."

"He shouldn't have taken you anywhere." Her brother's eyes remained fixed on Eric. "Do you have any idea who his father is, Hannah? He's scum, that's what. And I'm sure his spawn is no better."

Upset that her brother judged Eric on the basis of his father's reputation alone, Hannah approached and grabbed Josiah's sleeve, trying to pull his arm away from Eric. "You have no idea what you're talking about. What are you doing home anyhow? It's not Christmas break."

"I quit school."

"Quit?"

"I suggest we all go inside before the weather gets worse. Your sister needs to get dry, and I could do with a toweling off, too."

Josiah turned a fierce glare on Eric. "This isn't over."

"Yes," Hannah said just as adamantly. "It is."

Josiah glanced at Hannah then back to Eric before he

released him with a little shove. "Fine. Go inside. But we *will* talk later."

Hannah grabbed Eric's arm and pulled him to walk back with her to the house. She didn't wait to see what Josiah would do. She loved her brother, older by almost a year, but he could take the big-brother protectiveness a bit far.

"Don't mind him," she reassured Eric when they were in the mudroom. She peeled off her wet coat and scarf, as he did the same and tossed them over a chair. "He's got bigger problems when Daddy finds out he left school."

"I'm not worried. You should get into dry clothes. I'll do the same."

"Eric!" she called out before he could leave. He looked over his shoulder at her.

"I hope this doesn't mean. . .that is, I hope we're still on for your part of the deal, though mine was a complete washout."

At her little pun, he gave a full-blown smile that threatened to make her unsteady again. "Are you kidding? Be prepared to leave at six thirty Monday night so we can be on time for the town meeting at seven."

"Town meeting?" She barely curbed a groan. "I hear they're quite. . .long." And tedious. And monotonous. And every other boring word she could think of.

"You've never been. Why does that not surprise me? It's time you opened your eyes to what's going on in your community, Hannah."

"I can't wait," she replied with a forced smile.

"Cheer up." He gave her another irrepressible grin. "It might not turn out as badly as you think."

❧

Eric shed his damp clothes and toweled off, dressing in a pair of warm, dry trousers and a wool sweater. A loud knock threatened to take the door off its hinges.

Heaving a sigh, he opened it, not surprised to see Hannah's older brother glaring at him. He realized then that this was the young man's room, another reason for him to despise Eric.

"If you want me out, I can be gone in ten minutes."

Josiah narrowed his eyes. "I thought you promised my parents your *help*."

"I meant out of your room."

He scowled. "Like Mama would agree. You may have fooled her, but I know your kind. I have you figured out by a mile. And I know what your father is. A murderer, a con man, a rapist—"

"Past tense."

"Doesn't matter." Josiah punched his index finger in Eric's chest. "You've heard the old saying 'The apple doesn't fall far from the tree'? I'm wise to you. And now that I'm home, we don't need you around here anymore."

"Yet you just reminded me of the promise I made to your parents." Eric remained calm, though the man stepped on his every nerve and he felt like giving as good as he got. "If they want me out, I'll go. But with the damage to this house and winter waiting at the front door, I can't see that happening anytime soon. Can you?"

Josiah narrowed his eyes in clear hatred. "Just watch your back, Fontaine. And stay away from my sister! I'll be watching every move you make." He grimaced, turning away from the door.

Catching sight of David coming into the corridor from the stairwell, Eric gave the boy a friendly smile. David didn't smile back, his look suspicious as he moved toward Josiah, who clapped an arm around the boy's shoulders. Clearly Josiah had poisoned his little brother's mind against Eric.

Shaking his head, Eric closed the door and went to the bureau to pull out a pair of socks. Why did he stay where he wasn't wanted? He had nothing tying him to this place. Josiah seemed to think he could take over repairs, so why not let him? Why did the idea of leaving not appeal as it had a week before?

He had just tied his shoes when another knock, this one lighter, tapped at his door.

"Seems you're a popular man today," he muttered to himself as he rose from the bed and moved to admit his guest. Mrs. Thomas stood on the other side.

"I'm sorry to bother you. I would like a few moments to speak with you, if I may."

He smiled politely. "It's no bother." He waved an arm to the side. "Please, come in."

She did, and he remained standing at the open door.

"Hannah mentioned you've met my eldest son."

"Oui," Eric answered wryly. *If one could call it that.*

She sighed. "It is a sad situation, and I know it must be difficult for you that some people cannot look beyond past mistakes, choosing to judge a family for one man's sins. When loyalty comes into the balance, protecting loved ones can take on new meaning." She laid a hand on his shoulder, her eyes shining in sincerity. "I've had the advantage of spending my mornings getting to know you in our breakfast conversations. I see you are a good man. Your mother raised you with Christian ideals. I only wish my own children would learn them as well as you have."

Her praise eased the sting of Josiah's behavior. "Thanks for the vote of confidence. Besides Hannah, you're the only one who doesn't mind my presence here."

"Ah yes. My daughter." She grew pensive. "She's made many mistakes since living at my uncle's; and at the elite school she attended, she found the wrong friends. She was very young when we left the Refuge, once I learned my uncle was alive and had returned to Connecticut. But my uncle. . .he challenged my husband's and my ideas on raising our children, making us question our decisions and often going behind our backs to do the opposite of what we approved. Hannah has lived a very. . .privileged life these past five years. At the Refuge, all her needs were also met. She knows nothing of hardship. But she is smart." A reflective expression came into her eyes. "It often takes her time to come to a knowledge of the truth; she is young. But she does. And I sense you are a good influence for her."

He squinted in curiosity. "Exactly what are you saying, Mrs. Thomas?"

"I heard my son's parting words. I do not agree with Josiah. You have my blessing to befriend my daughter."

He regarded her skeptically. "And your husband supports the idea?" During one of their breakfast conversations, Eric had admitted to her that he'd overheard her conversation with Mr. Thomas.

"I will speak with my husband. Please understand, he acts out of fear from all that has happened to us connected with the Piccoli mob. Your father was part of that ring of terror and created his own as well. Also, being bedridden has not helped my husband's attitude. But if Bill knew you as I have come to know you, I do not feel he would be so. . .hesitant."

Eric could think of a better word for her husband's treatment of him but respectfully nodded. "I plan on taking Hannah to the town meeting next week."

"The town meeting?" Her surprise was evident.

"I thought seeing the day-to-day issues of what's happening in the world, in this case her own little community, might be an eye-opening experience. She mentioned she hopes to be a writer. Attending a meeting like that could be helpful."

Mrs. Thomas smiled. "Oh, no doubt. Your plan sounds like a worthy one."

Eric thought so, too, but couldn't help grin at thinking what Hannah's reaction might be.

eight

Mere boredom couldn't begin to describe Hannah's feelings as she listened to the secretary read the minutes from the last meeting. For the time period of the novel Hannah was writing, she might use *tedium, dreariness, insipidness*—the French would describe it as *ennui*. A much more sophisticated sound.

Eric leaned to whisper near her ear, "So what do you think?"

"It's lovely." She smiled and noticed a faint grin edge his mouth.

"Well, I don't know if I would call a draft lovely."

"Draft?"

He lifted an eyebrow at her puzzlement. "I asked if you were cold, with the way you keep rubbing your arms, and asked if you want to move closer."

"Oh, that." She felt a flush of warmth now. "Closer—no! I mean, I'm fine, just. . .lovely," she finished off her excuse in a weak manner. The time spent sitting beside Eric and making easy conversation before the meeting itself had been quite lovely. She wondered if she could interest him in a stroll in the park on their way home then felt amazed at the idea. She, who never liked to walk anywhere, was considering one? But to extend their night, alone, and have more time to talk, she would reconsider her former views of the activity.

"These public meetings can be a little dull at first, when they go over items already mentioned, but give them time to get to the grittier issues. You might learn something."

Learn something? Learn what? How to paralyze a person with ennui in under ten minutes? She stifled a giggle at the thought. When the chairperson went into discussion for the funds to fix one of the covered bridges and all the *yea*-ing and *nay*-ing the vote entailed from those gathered, she felt hard-pressed not to yawn. Suddenly she heard her name mentioned. Shocked, she sat up rigid, as if a teacher had caught her nodding off in class.

"Our own Miss Thomas is with us tonight, a rising young talent who will both write and direct the play being presented for our Founder's Day extravaganza."

Hannah realized then that the subject had moved from reparation of the bridge to the upcoming community celebration. She smiled, giving a nervous nod to the speaker, who stared directly at her, and hoped the man had no idea she felt adrift in the conversation.

"Miss Thomas, would you care to share a few words about your project?"

No, she wouldn't. She really wouldn't. . . .

She gave a stiff nod and clutched the empty chair in front of her as a sea of faces turned her way to look at her on the second-to-last row. She felt them blur, then chided herself. She had once wanted to be an actress. Certainly she could address these people on a matter dear to her heart.

She filled them in on the foundation of her idea, noting a few nods of approval, which gave her the boost of courage needed. She fielded questions, delighted at the interest shown and at the offer of a few volunteers to help with the set.

When the meeting drew to a close, she was fairly glowing with their praise, but Eric seemed strangely distant, as if not happy with the outcome of the meeting.

"Shall we take a walk in the park?" she asked hopefully, after the last of the attendees had come up to offer words of encouragement or introductions. "It's close."

"I don't think so. It's nearing ten now, and tomorrow is Sunday."

"Sunday?"

"Church."

"Oh right."

He glanced her way, but she averted her eyes. She went to church every week, listened to the preacher, did everything that was required of a Christian. Feeling ill at ease, she looked his way. "What?"

He shook his head. "I'm only trying to figure you out."

"Meaning?"

"When there's talk of movies and your play, you light up like a firefly. But when the subject turns to God, you tend to clam up. I've seen you do it with your mother and once when I brought up my family's mission and the testimonies given there."

She shrugged a little self-consciously and looked around the area. "Can we go? We're almost the last ones to leave."

They left the building, but in the car, she brought up the subject again, unnerved by the unnatural silence that had descended since he last spoke.

"It's not that I don't believe in God." She pulled at the tips of her gloves. "I've been raised on the teachings of Christ. But, well, Julia and Muffy tend to think that the Bible is more of a history book of. . .stories. None of it really. . .life-pressing."

"That's a strange way to put it, since scripture deals with each solitary life and what will become of it based on the decisions we make."

"Oh, I know my friends don't have all the answers, but. . . I don't know." She shrugged, unable to express her thoughts clearly.

"I think I do." His voice came solemn, and he glanced her way, his eyes a little sad, before he looked back at the road. "You've never really suffered. You don't know what it's like to reach rock bottom and need God as desperately as you need air and water, because you've had everything handed to you since you were old enough to understand the world. And the world you understand is a place of privilege and wealth."

His words hit too close to home for comfort. She couldn't

remember ever being denied anything, except, of course, to go back to her great-uncle's to live. "You're pitying me?" she asked in shock. After all, his family seemed to be the ones struggling to make ends meet. If her father ever needed money, all he had to do was ask her great-uncle.

"In a way, maybe I am."

"Well don't!"

"Sorry, can't help myself. In this past week I've come to care about your welfare, *mon amie*, and by that I mean your ultimate welfare. Of your soul."

His words disconcerted her, though she clung to his first ones. And delivered in the language of love, no less. He cared about her!

"You know a lot of French, don't you?"

He looked at her strangely. "My father is from France. It is my second language."

"Right." She knew that. Why had she asked something so obvious?

"In our household both languages are spoken; my mother is also fluent in it. And I find myself sometimes fluctuating between the two when I speak."

"Oh, don't misunderstand me. I like it." She smiled, adopting a sweeter attitude to carry through with her plan. She turned a little on the seat to look at him, batting her lashes as she'd seen Muffy do. "You really are such a gentleman, Eric. I'm sorry I got upset. I don't know what got into me."

"Is something in your eye?"

"My eye? No, it's fine." She stopped her rapid blinking, now embarrassed, and cleared her throat. "I was wondering, though."

"Yes?"

"Since my plan for a good time was a complete failure, I would like a second shot."

"What do you have in mind?"

He seemed leery, which made her wonder what she had

said to cause his abrupt distance this time. "How about a movie? At least if it rains, it won't be a loss since we'll have the theater roof over our heads. A favorite of mine is still playing at the movie house, though I imagine they'll take it down soon."

He hesitated so long that she feared he might decline her invitation. "All right," he said at last. "Next weekend then?"

"Can't it be sooner?"

He gave her another swift glance. "I do have your house to work on, remember."

"Right. Of course. Next Saturday then." She forced a smile, hoping for the days to fly. . .well, at least six of them.

All through the following week, Eric tried to keep his mind on his work and less on the feisty brunette who seemed determined to help him. Their conversation on the way home from the meeting had sparked warnings in his mind. He found himself not only hoping she would see the danger in her cavalier attitude toward God and the Christian faith, but desperately wanting her to understand. Yet she wasn't the only one acting carelessly.

While her mother might approve if he were to take an interest in Hannah, her father and brother still considered him an irredeemable danger to the family. But the almost palpable tension in the house was now targeted toward Josiah and his decision to quit school. From Eric's room, it had been impossible to ignore Mr. Thomas's voice raised from the adjacent bedroom as he confronted his son with his "foolish choice." Josiah had countered, just as loudly, that he planned to earn a living with his roommate friend from college, working on his father's boat as a fisherman, an admission Josiah's father hadn't taken well. Hannah had been quiet ever since, clearly affected by the family tension—another reason Eric felt sorry for her and didn't refuse her laughable excuse for help. As far as any true interest went, he had no intention of taking their relationship any further than friendship.

Hannah intrigued and baffled him. Certainly that must be the reason he couldn't stop thinking of her. She was like a paper chain of people his little sisters were fond of making—entertaining but flimsy, a long line of cutout fictional characters that didn't depict her true nature—the cutouts the only parts of her persona Hannah seemed willing to display to the world, as if it were her audience. But at times, in the unexpected warmth of her smile or the sincerity of her illuminating words, he'd detected more. Hidden deep within, he sensed the original cowered, a woman of gentle sensitivity shielding an insecure little girl. Hurting. Restless. Perhaps she'd buried her real feelings so deep she didn't realize they existed. On the other hand, his emotions always seemed to surface. He'd witnessed more than his share of suffering and hopelessness growing up in the mission, and the Depression only made matters worse.

In one matter they shared a common bond. He sensed Hannah sought the same peace he did—a need for serenity. That link made him want to help her, even befriend her. He missed the times of togetherness with his huge family and assumed that's why he'd agreed to Hannah's outings for "fun."

When Saturday again rolled around, he waited in the parlor for her to join him for the matinee. He wondered, though, since she'd already seen the movie, why she would want to see it again.

Her footsteps on the top landing had him look up, just as the doorbell rang. He looked in surprise at the door a few feet from him.

"Would you mind getting that, Eric?" Hannah sounded out of breath. "I forgot my scarf. I won't be but a moment."

Eric felt odd greeting whoever stood on the other side, since it wasn't his home, but he put on a charming smile and swung open the door.

"*Bonjour,*" he said to a handsome-looking woman who

appeared to be the same age as Hannah's mother. Next to her stood a younger woman, both of them with blazing red hair. "I'm Eric Fontaine, a guest of the Thomases. How can I be of service to you ladies?"

The older woman turned a pasty gray, her mouth dropping open in horrified shock. "No!" she rasped out in a whisper. Her green eyes grew huge in terror before her lids suddenly fluttered and closed. Eric barely caught her before she could sink all the way to the ground in a dead faint or hit the baby carriage the young woman rolled.

"Mama!" the girl cried, grabbing her arm. "Mama, what's wrong?"

"We need to get her inside, out of this cold wind." Eric had no idea who the woman was, but he couldn't leave her inert on the doorstep. He managed to shift her into his arms, glad he'd kept in shape, the strain on his muscles taxing as he lifted and carried her into the house. The other woman followed. In the parlor, he laid the older woman on the couch and knelt beside her, putting his fingers to her neck to check her pulse.

"What are you doing?" a man's deep voice suddenly boomed. "Get your hands off my wife!" Eric turned to see a tall and husky, silver-haired gentleman hurry into the parlor. The man stopped suddenly at the sight of his face. "No. It can't be—it's impossible."

"What's impossible, Papa?" The young woman moved to her father, grabbing his arm as if she might try to stop him from throwing a punch at Eric, though the man appeared paralyzed in his tracks as if he'd forgotten his earlier angst. She looked back and forth between them. "Do you know this man?" she whispered. "He said his name is Eric Fontaine."

Her father's eyes widened farther as if he'd seen a ghost. "Impossible. . .you, you haven't aged in all this time?"

Eric instantly understood. "My father is Eric Fontaine Sr. I'm his son." And he understood in an instant the identity of the unconscious woman, recalling the redhead his father told them he had wronged.

Hannah came into the parlor, her expression puzzled. "Clemmie?" Her welcoming smile faltered when she noticed the woman on the sofa. "What happened to your mother?" She looked up. "Eric?"

"A case of mistaken identity."

"Is it?" Josiah suddenly appeared through the door. "Or maybe she sensed the evil of your father in you."

Mrs. Thomas hurried past her son, as if she'd been privy to the whole incident, a small jar in her hand. "Stand aside, please."

Eric stood up from kneeling beside the sofa and watched her lift the woman's head, bringing the jar under her nose. The woman recoiled as she got a whiff of the smelling salts, and her eyes fluttered open. They latched onto Eric. "You. . . how?" she said hoarsely as her husband came to her side and she leaned against him in support.

"Non, madame," he said quickly. "I'm not who you think."

"You. . .you said you're Eric F–Fontaine."

"Oui. Named for my father. I'm his son."

"But. . ." She pulled her brows together in confusion. "You look so much like. . .like he did. On the *Titanic*. You could be him. Looking at you, it's as if. . ." Her breath came tense. "As if you never aged. As if you've. . .come back. . . ."

"Charleigh, sweetheart." Her husband took her hand in his and patted it. "It's not Eric." He directed an uncertain glance his way. "At least not the Eric we knew."

"I think we should go." Hannah came to stand beside Eric.

"Yes, I think that would be wise."

Charleigh cast a rapid glance back and forth between daughter and mother. "You don't mean. . . Sarah, tell me you're not actually letting him take Hannah out?"

"Mother." Josiah took Charleigh's side. "Are you crazy? You can't let Hannah go with him!"

Eric felt weary of the entire situation, tired of being judged for his father's past sins, especially by veritable strangers. "Despite what you remember about my father, he is a changed man. The man I've heard about since I've come to your town is a stranger to me. He's nothing like the person who raised me, I assure you, and I'm nothing like the person he was."

"We really should go or we'll be late." Hannah looked from Eric to the young woman. "We'll talk later."

Taking hold of Eric's arm, she walked with him out of the parlor, ignoring Josiah, who scowled at them both.

nine

Outside, Hannah vented her anger.

"They have no right to judge you!"

Taken aback by the vehemence of her low words and how her eyes flashed like hard steel, he shook his head, still stunned. "That's the woman my father abused on the *Titanic*, isn't it? The one he wronged in so many ways."

Hannah winced. "Yes. I heard about the awful things he did to Aunt Charleigh, and I'm not excusing any of it. But I happen to know that every one of those people inside have done terrible things for which they have good reason to be ashamed."

"My father warned me this might happen. That though your father and the others had visited the mission that day, over a decade ago, and made an uneasy sort of peace, they'd been wary of him. He thought they might later have questioned if his conversion were only a trick, another con, since he'd been a master of deception. Of course he had no idea when he asked me to come to Connecticut that I would run into your aunt and uncle here." He sighed. "And I'm sure they never thought they would see a Fontaine again. Especially outside of New York."

"I don't care. It's still not right. They expect mercy, but they won't give your father the same benefit, believing he can change, too? That's just. . .wrong! And why in the world should they take all this out on you? You weren't even *alive* when any of it happened. Just because you look like your father? That's a pathetic excuse. You've never done anything to warrant such treatment. Aunt Charleigh—okay, yes, I can understand her shocked reaction, but Josiah's hostility, I can't.

He barely knows you and hasn't even met your father—"

"Hannah." Eric grasped her shoulders to get her to look at him and try to calm her. "It's all right." He smiled. "You're a sweet young woman to care, but don't get yourself so upset over this. I don't want to be the cause of anything that would alienate you from your family."

The fire left her eyes, her expression almost sad, making him curious, but she nodded.

On the drive to town, she didn't say much, and he found himself frequently glancing her way to make sure she was okay. What had caused such a change?

The movie house was in need of repairs like so many places, but tickets weren't expensive, the seats were comfortable, and he wore a coat so he didn't feel the chill inside the massive theater. Once the curtain opened, a short newsreel played onscreen, optimistic human-interest stories set amid the nation's suffering along with a short reel of President Roosevelt waving to a crowd while the voice-over mentioned the war in Europe and the munitions being made in Connecticut to aid the Allies. At this, a few young men in the audience gave a loud hurrah, instantly hushed by the people with them. Eric smiled at their enthusiasm, now understanding how Hannah had come by the information. He wasn't sure how he felt about the war in general, though what the power-hungry Hitler did was clearly wrong. But Eric was amazed that such an informative reel, however short, would be shown in a theater.

Another short, this time a slapstick reel, had many men gasping in laughter, followed by the main feature that brought the women to tears. Toward the end, Hannah sniffled with regularity, and Eric offered her his handkerchief, though his vision had become a bit blurred, too.

"Thank you," she whispered, taking it and dabbing at her eyes.

The picture, about a spoiled, wealthy socialite with an incurable brain disease, who sacrificed her last living minutes with her husband to send him off on his preplanned trip that would boost his career as a doctor, her first truly selfless act and her last, surprised Eric. For one, the content matter didn't seem like something Hannah might choose. He had thought she would prefer something silly or flighty, though from what he'd read of it, *Gone with the Wind* couldn't be classified as either, and he remembered her mentioning that being her favorite novel. The subject matter of the current movie drama could even be considered moralistic, the woman changing for the better due to the love of one good man who had faith in her and saw something in her others didn't. The "victory" perhaps wasn't so "dark" as the title suggested.

"Bette Davis is just so amazing," Hannah gushed once they left the theater. "I could feel her sorrow and angst at the end, couldn't you? Though she covered up her feelings with a smile so her husband wouldn't suspect she'd gone blind and the end was near. Oh, I hope I can write a novel like that. It's my fondest dream, though of course first I had hoped to go to Hollywood and be an actress—or even Broadway—but Mother and Daddy didn't approve and have never let me even visit New York."

She stopped for a breath, and he used the opportunity to speak. "It's a nice afternoon. Would you like to take a walk?" He hoped to avoid the Lyons company and felt if he drew out his and Hannah's time together, chances were strong the family wouldn't be present upon their return.

Her eyes twinkled. "I'd love to walk with you."

The town green was only a few blocks' distant, and they reached the area in less than five minutes. Towering cedars and maples provided some shade, though soon the leaves of the maples would fall to the ground in a shower of color.

"See that old building?" She pointed to a colonial house in the distance. "That's where we'll be holding the play. Oh, I hope you'll still be here. And there's our church."

He followed her gaze toward the familiar white steeple on

the far side of the green, nestled amid clusters of trees.

"My best friend, Clemmie, married there. One day I hope to have my wedding there, too."

At the wistful quality of her voice, Eric felt a little awkward.

"Clemmie. . .the woman who came to visit?"

"Yes."

"Maybe I shouldn't have taken you away. We could have done this another time."

"Are you serious?" She laughed wryly. "I wanted out of there as much as you did. Though Clemmie didn't say anything, she might have, and I didn't want to hear it. Her mother wasn't the only victim of. . ." She hesitated.

"My father," Eric put in steadily.

"Yes, well. . .Joel, Clemmie's husband, he was a victim, too."

Eric pondered her words. "I don't remember Father talking about a Joel. Charleigh and Stewart and a woman named Darcy are the ones I heard the most about."

She brightened. "Oh, you would love Aunt Darcy. Everyone does. Now there's a woman who's not afraid to speak her mind, regardless of what people think." Eric wondered if she wished she could classify herself in the same mold. "Joel was a boy when he ran across your father at a carnival. Your father wanted to make him an accomplice, since Joel was very good at cons and worked for his father, who died in prison—but I'm rambling again. Sorry." She offered a penitent smile. "Joel was, I think, twelve when your father used him to gain admittance to Lyons Refuge. His plan was to gain revenge on everyone there, and he held a gun on Aunt Charleigh and Aunt Darcy, threatening Joel if he wouldn't help."

"He wanted the diamonds, too," Eric put in, having heard the story many times.

"Yes." Hannah looked at him in surprise, as if amazed he would know that. "I didn't learn everything until Clemmie told me years ago, but he and Aunt Charleigh worked together to steal an heirloom diamond necklace from Lady

Annabelle when they sailed the *Titanic*."

"And your aunt Charleigh, then known as Charlotte, changed her name to Myra, hoping to evade my father," Eric continued solemnly. "He found her and demanded she give him the necklace and come back to him, but your uncle Stewart saved her. So he bided his time and returned to the Refuge when the opportunity arose and your uncle was out of town. But Darcy's husband surprised him, and it ended with my father getting shot and later going to prison."

She stopped walking and looked at him. "You know the story well."

"I spent my lifetime being raised on it. Father spoke of the boy, but I didn't know his name was Joel. I also didn't know who the Lyonses actually were until they and their friends came to the mission that day and I overheard them talking. I was eight at the time."

Hannah hesitated, as if unsure she should speak. "How do you feel about all of it? About him?"

Eric thought about how to answer. "When I grew old enough to realize the enormity of my father's crimes and that he'd lied to Charleigh about them being married for three years—arranging a fake ceremony—then on that last night, hours before the *Titanic* sank, abusing her in his jealousy and leaving her to die. . .when I understood all that, I hated him." He shook his head in remembered confusion. "But I loved him, too. I loved the man I *knew*, not the monster he described. It was difficult to equate the two conflicting parts of one man, and I couldn't understand how he could love my mother so deeply yet hurt a woman so horribly as he had Charleigh. It's no wonder she fainted upon seeing me. People often tell me I look just like my father when he was younger."

"I never saw him, but I still say they shouldn't take his past out on you."

"It's been difficult, I won't lie to you. But I better under-stand their hesitance to trust me when it seems to them that my father has come to life before their eyes, the way he used to look at the time of his cons."

She considered that. "I see your point. At least your parents share the truth with you and don't hide things you ought to know."

At her bitter words, he regarded her somberly. "Sometimes it's better not knowing the past, mon amie. It took me a long time to be able to look at my father without loathing him once I fully began to understand all he'd done. I marveled that they let him out of prison at all! They couldn't prove many of his early crimes, so he didn't receive the long sentence he deserved. Perhaps also that his father was a *comte* had some bearing on the matter. Now he has the title."

She blinked in clear shock. "Your father is a French count? I had no idea. So that makes you a *vicomte*?"

He chuckled. "It's not such a big thing as it was in the nineteenth century, but oui. Before my father changed his name, it was Fontaneau."

It was a moment before she spoke again. "So what changed your mind about him?"

"My mother." He smiled sadly.

"You miss them."

"At times, yes. I would look at my mother, who seemed the closest thing to a saint I'd known, and wonder how she could love such a man. But she does. It's in every word she says to him, every look she gives, every time she touches him. She saw the worth no one else tried to, with the exception of her family, and he became a better man because of their faith in him."

"Something like Judith in *Dark Victory*."

He grinned in resignation. "*Something* like that. Mother pulled me aside one day, questioning why I would no longer speak to my father. Once I told her, she looked at me sternly and asked, 'Eric Joseph, do you consider yourself better than God?' I was thirteen and had just read about Lucifer, who thought himself better than God and waged a war against

Him. So I was naturally appalled, thinking my dear sainted mother must think I was as bad as the devil." He chuckled wryly. "She said something that stuck with me through the years and helped me learn to judge no man as a lost cause, which can be very helpful when your family runs a mission. She said, 'Paul was a murderer, David an adulterer, Jacob a thief, and Peter a liar. If God could forgive every one of those men their sins and raise them to be mighty men of God, who are you to say He shouldn't or couldn't? He's a God of lost causes and is glorified when people watch the impossible accomplished right before their eyes.'"

Hannah smiled. "Your mother sounds a lot like mine." She tilted her head in curiosity. "How did your parents meet, anyhow?"

"The guard who kept watch over the cell block at the prison where my father stayed quoted scripture to him, even read from it. My father never forgot how Charleigh came to him before the police arrived and forgave him and how Darcy gave him money to buy a coat. No one had ever done anything nice for him, and their actions helped to soften his heart, so that he was open to hear the message of the gospel. His enemies repaid him with kindness, and he couldn't fathom it. Eventually, the guard led my father to Christ, and the two became friends. That guard was my uncle Joseph. After my father was released, my uncle invited him to a family dinner, and my mother was there."

"Weren't her parents upset or worried when your father took an interest in her?"

"Oh yes. Father had to prove himself before they would let him be alone in the same room with her, but they gave him that chance. They didn't just assume he could never change and treat him badly, as many had done, no matter how he tried to make amends. He came to work for my grandfather when the mission was hardly as big or as productive as it is now. My father had ideas that made it that way. Soon my grandfather saw he wasn't only brilliant, but also trustworthy. He gave the management of the mission over to my father a year after meeting him. Shortly after that, he gave his blessing for him and Mother to marry."

"That's just so. . .romantic."

At her dreamy sigh, he lifted his brows. "Romantic?"

"Oh yes. How she stuck by his side, how she had faith in him despite the odds and the mind-sets of those around them. . ."

Before she could go off into one of her dream-world soliloquies, he felt a sharp tug at the back of his coat. He turned, Hannah also stopping to look, and noticed a little girl in a drab blue dress and shabby coat, both which looked as if they could do with a washing. Her brown hair appeared clean though straggled, her face heartbreakingly thin.

"Please, mister, can you spare a dime?"

He took into account how snugly her dress fit, her ribs poking through the folds.

"When have you eaten last?"

She looked startled by his gentle question and wrinkled her brow. "We found some food in the bin behind the coffee shop yesterday."

"We?"

"My little brother and me." She looked at the shrubbery and waved in signal for someone to join her. The bushes rustled, and a small boy, possibly five, came out. His eyes, the same shade of brown as the girl's, seemed to take up most of his freckled face. "My mama got real bad sick," the girl went on to explain. "She lost her job at the mercantile. She's sick now."

"And your father?"

"He left when things got bad."

A strong twinge of sympathy made Eric hunch down and put his hands to her shoulders. "How would you like a hot meal from that coffee shop over there?" He pointed down the street.

Her eyes shone as if he'd promised her the moon and stars. "Really?" She glanced at the boy, a head shorter than herself, and took his hand. "Jimmy, too?"

Eric smiled at the boy. "Jimmy, too."

"Golly, mister, that'd be swell!"

Eric glanced at Hannah, whose expression looked a little odd, but she didn't disagree. During the entire walk to the shop, with the children following as quiet as church mice behind, Hannah didn't say a word, and to his surprise, Eric really wished to know what she was thinking.

ten

Hannah sat next to Eric, across from the children, who ate their hot soup as enthusiastically as if it were ice cream. She thought of her little brother, who turned up his nose at any form of liquid nourishment, and his informative boast to Eric of their daily intake of desserts at her great-uncle's. She wondered what Eric must think of her family. It was bad enough he'd called her a "sweet young woman." Reminded of her foolish bet with Julia and Muffy to win him over, she could hardly be considered sweet.

But more than her twinge of conscience for her lack of ethics, seeing evidence of the starvation that had plagued her town affected her strongly. To see children as young as Abbie forced to beg in the park for a meal had horrified her and pulled at her heartstrings. She knew that many in her state now had work, but apparently the suffering still existed. How had she not known or seen it? True, they now lived in a rural area and her great-uncle's mansion had been situated in the more affluent district, but not to realize the situation baffled Hannah. Were there more out there like Shirley and Jimmy? There must be, since Eric had mentioned children who'd been thrown onto the streets, children his family's mission had helped.

She sipped her coffee, having declined Eric's offer of a meal, and watched the brother and sister wolf down their roast beef sandwiches. Oddly, she felt more satisfied watching them eat than partaking of food herself. When they dug into their slabs of apple pie with equal gusto, she worried they might get tummy aches from so much good food all at once.

Once the children were satisfied, Eric ordered more

sandwiches and asked the waitress to wrap them, telling her he'd pay for everything. Hannah found herself wondering where Eric had obtained so much money and asked him about it once he handed Shirley the sandwiches, with the promise from the child to take them home to their mother, the box containing enough for all three to share in two meals.

"Father didn't want me to. . .tarnish my welcome. He also didn't anticipate your mother's invitation to me as a guest in your home."

"Then your parents are wealthy?"

"Let's just say we're not poor and leave it at that."

Clearly, he didn't wish to speak of it, and Hannah wondered if their money was part of what Eric's father had received during his life of crime or in his inheritance as a count. She found it baffling that Eric's roots also stemmed from nobility. And after coming to America, Eric Sr. had also worked for a gangster. *Like Daddy did. . .*

Hannah still hadn't approached her father with what she knew. She realized she should reconcile her feelings toward him, now knowing of his criminal history, as Eric had done with his father. Yet everything she had learned since she first opened the door to Eric Jr. and he had walked across their threshold still was too much to process, and she remained silent on their return home.

Rescuer—yes. Rogue? At times. . .handyman, vicomte. . . *And what else?*

Once they stepped inside the house, she almost groaned when she heard Aunt Charleigh's precise British accent drift from the parlor. She had hoped their visitors would be gone, not wishing Eric to perhaps suffer through further mistreatment.

They approached the parlor, and she sensed his tension.

Aunt Charleigh rose from the sofa when she noticed him. Instead of excusing herself and leaving, she surprised Hannah by moving their way and stopping in front of Eric. Again her eyes made a sweeping perusal, the intense shock on her face to look at his evident.

"I owe you an apology for my behavior." Her smile came polite, if shaky. "I skipped breakfast this morning in my eagerness to arrive in Connecticut and visit my daughter and her family, which in all likelihood aided my swoon."

"Under the circumstances, you owe me no apologies, Mrs. Lyons." He hesitated, as if he had more to say but wasn't sure if he should. "My father told me he'd never been taught to love because he'd never known it. His mother ran away with another man when he was very small, and his father took his anger out on him, also condemning his mother and the institute of marriage—why my father never went through with an actual marriage to you. His father led him not to believe in it. Despite his status as a comte's son, he had little, and he learned to think that to love something meant to possess it. In that sense, he came to care for you and told me that's why he always found it so difficult to let you go and searched for you to get you back. It wasn't just about the cons. But he was a mass of contradictions and ended up giving in to his rages and jealousy, treating you horribly, just as his father had done to him. He didn't know how to stop."

"Oh my. . ." Her face lost a little color, and tears glossed her eyes.

Uncle Stewart protectively moved to her side. "Why are you telling us this?"

"I think it's time Mrs. Lyons knew everything my father never could say and wished to, and then after he found Christ and love with my mother, never had an opportunity to tell her. Forgive me if I spoke out of turn, but since I've taken the brunt of his mistakes since I got here, I felt like the perfect liaison to speak. Now if you'll excuse me, I'll bid you *bon nuit.*"

Everyone gaped as he left the room.

"Hannah?" At her mother's voice, she blinked, looking away from the now empty doorway. "Will you please get more tea, dear? I think everyone could use a cup."

Hannah vaguely nodded, glancing at her aunt, whose shocked dismay was still apparent. In the kitchen, she poured herself a cup first, feeling in limbo. At a step behind her, she glanced over her shoulder to see her redheaded friend.

"If you've come to criticize Eric, save your breath, Clemmie. Maybe he shouldn't have said all that, but I'm glad he did."

"I'm the last person to offer any kind of speech. Joel was once the bad boy of the bunch, remember."

Hannah swung around to face her. "But Eric's not. That's the point. He's done nothing to warrant anyone's bad treatment. *Nothing.*"

Clemmie's green eyes narrowed in enlightenment, and self-consciously Hannah looked away. "Those are rather strong words in defense of someone who's only a visiting guest. . .or is he more than that, Hannah?"

"I don't know what you mean."

"I think you do." Clemmie approached, putting her arm around Hannah's shoulders. "Just be careful. I'd hate to see you get hurt."

Hannah winced, sure if Clemmie knew the particulars and the foolish little challenge to win Eric's favor, she would be hearing a different sort of speech.

"I'll admit, knowing that the son of the man who abused my mother is in your house—staying here—well, yes, I'm still a bit shocked and anxious. But if anyone knows how God can change hearts, I do. I'm sure Eric's father is nothing like the man Mama knew. Just from hearing Eric's admirable defense of him, I can tell that."

"Then why tell me to be careful?"

"Because you seem to be moving too fast. The way you behave, you sound like a woman in love, fighting for her man, and you've scarcely known him, what, two weeks?"

"In love?" Hannah stared at her friend in utter disbelief. "That's preposterous. I don't love Eric." She gave an incredulous huff of laughter. "But he has become a friend, and I don't like to see my friends mistreated."

Which is why you're engaging in such a demeaning bet, her conscience maliciously whispered.

"I don't want to talk about this anymore." Hannah set the teapot on the tray. "Were you able to locate anyone to make costumes for the play? I admit I've had nightmares of the little colonists and Indians running around naked in pilgrim hats and feather headdresses."

Clemmie laughed. "I assure you, we'll have something for the children to wear even if I have to try my own hand at sewing. I don't think Thea would approve of her two little girls running around in their underthings. How's the play coming along?"

"Oh, all right." She didn't admit that, since Eric's stay, she hadn't managed to concentrate long enough to add the second act.

"Maybe we can help. Joel has an old typewriter he said he was willing to give you. He was given a nicer one for his job at the newspaper office, so he has a spare."

"Oh, that would be splendid." And surely all her stories would progress much faster!

"I'll bring it Wednesday."

"Then we're still on?"

"Of course we're still on," Clemmie said with a reassuring laugh. "I would never break the tradition of our monthly standing lunch dates."

"Good. But no more warnings about Eric, all right?"

"Honey, I'm just concerned. Much like you were with me when Joel was blind and I pretended to be a stranger, to help him, so he wouldn't kick me to the curb."

"That was entirely different. You've always loved Joel, ever since we were children."

"True. But I can't help think there's more beneath the surface with you and Eric."

"And I've told you there's not, so there's no reason for concern." She managed a smile, her face warming, and quickly averted her attention to the task of gathering teacups.

❧

Eric spent the next two days working on the loose wiring in the upstairs corridor. Hannah kept herself strangely absent, which surprised and oddly disappointed him. He knew she'd gone to lunch with Clemmie yesterday, after explaining to him they always met on the fifteenth of each month to catch up on their lives. Today she was home. He just wasn't sure where.

Had he really begun to rely on her companionship so much that he missed her absence? He supposed that shouldn't come as a surprise. Eric had never been a loner, always surrounded by family and those at the mission. These past weeks at the Thomas residence had been a lesson in tolerance, in being treated as an outcast.

"Whatcha doin'?"

Abbie came up behind him. He looked over his shoulder at her shadowed form before turning back to his work, almost happy to see the precocious child, even if she did tend to addle his nerves with her personal questions.

"Fixing wires."

"Can I help?"

"Non. It's too dangerous for a little thing like you."

"I'm not so little." A pout angered her voice. "I go to school now like everyone else."

"But school doesn't teach you these kinds of things, and I don't want to see you get electrocuted."

"Aw, I never get to do anything fun around here."

Eric shook his head in amusement at her idea of fun.

"You and Hannah won't let me patch up walls, either."

"Your mother doesn't think the powder used for the paste would be good for your lungs since you've been sick. Besides, a lot of it is too high for you to reach."

"I can climb a ladder, too!"

Eric decided to let the matter drop, realizing Abbie wouldn't be satisfied. The silence lasted no more than several seconds.

"You like my sister, don't you? I mean *really* like her?"

He jerked in shock at the blunt question and pulled the pliers away, deciding if he didn't want to slip and electrocute himself or pull the wrong wire, he should quit until Abbie left. He'd cut the power supply to the upstairs but didn't trust the old wiring. "Your sister is a nice girl." He purposely was evasive. Moving to his feet, he clicked off the flashlight in his other hand. The window at the end of the corridor provided enough muted lighting to be able to see.

"Hey—where are you going?" Abbie complained as she followed him to the head of the stairs.

"Time for a coffee break." He took the steps, hearing her lighter tread behind him.

"There isn't any coffee left. Hannah's friends drank it all."

So Hannah's friends were here. That explained her distance.

"I heard them talking. About you. They don't think you like Hannah much."

Abbie's matter-of-fact statement made Eric pause on the stairwell near the banister Hannah had come flying down when he'd caught her.

"She told them you do."

"Did she?" Eric narrowed his eyes in curious thought and resumed walking to the landing.

"I think you like her, too."

He turned to face her. "Don't you have homework?"

"Why is everyone always asking me that?"

He hid a smile. "Guess they don't want you to fail."

She sighed. "Oh, all right. . ." Mumbling, she took the stairs back up to her room.

With coffee no longer an option, he decided to make a second visit to the library shelves. He'd left Hannah's Civil War novel upstairs but didn't really want to return to his room to get it. He was halfway finished with the story, which hadn't turned out so bad, after all.

He'd no more than turned the handle and pushed the door aside when he realized his mistake.

Julia and Muffy turned, looks of pleased surprise spreading over their features. Hannah sat behind a typewriter on the desk, bright spots of color blooming in her cheeks. The three looked as if they'd been immersed in an intense confrontation. Hannah's lashes swept downward in apparent nervousness, and Eric wondered if he'd been the topic.

"Sorry to interrupt. I'll just go—"

"Don't be silly." Julia approached before he could make his escape, a not so subtle sway to her hips. All that was missing was a long cigarette holder dangling from her fingers along with the vamp look. "We were wondering what had become of you."

Muffy trapped him from the other side, batting her lashes and smiling. "You really shouldn't work *all* the time. Come talk with us awhile. We were just finishing up."

Eric politely smiled at them, not wanting to offend Hannah's friends. He glanced her way, catching her fixed gaze on him. Her cheeks blossomed a deeper shade of rose.

"I really don't have the time." But neither girl would relent. Each of them took one of his arms, drawing him into the room.

"You're coming to the presentation next week, aren't you?" Muffy asked.

"Presentation?" He shook his head in confusion.

"The play, of course!" The short brunette gave an exuberant giggle. "After all the time we've spent working on this, you simply must come."

"It *is* for a worthy cause," Julia added. "The Founder's Day celebration will have a drive to help aid the destitute, and Hannah did mention your family supports that kind of thing."

He wondered just what Hannah had told them, his eyes

again going to hers. Again she quickly averted her gaze.

"Hannah did mention her project. I haven't decided if I'll attend or not."

He didn't miss the quick lift of Hannah's head or the injured look in her eyes.

"But you simply *must* come," Muffy urged, pulling on his arm, which she had yet to release. "There will be other things there to do, and food besides. It will be a lovely way for you to meet everyone, since most of the town will turn out for the event, I daresay."

"Yes," Julia agreed with an amused drawl. "Muffy's mother is in charge of food preparation. Their entire family has an overzealous fondness for indulging, so I'm certain there will be quite an enormous spread."

Muffy pulled her brows together in hurt at Julia's catty remark.

Eric had had enough.

"If you ladies will excuse me, I really need to get back to work."

"Surely it can wait a little longer?" Julia asked, affronted, as if she held some power over him.

"Actually, it can't." With one last glance at Hannah, who earnestly studied the paper in the typewriter, he left and returned upstairs.

No more than ten minutes passed before he heard her light tread on the stairwell. He didn't turn around to see. He didn't need to. She moved to his side and knelt down beside him.

"What are you doing?" she asked.

He glanced at her then focused back on his work. "Trying to fix this wiring, but your father should hire an electrician. My uncle taught me what he knew, but I'm no expert."

"Oh, but I most certainly disagree." Her words ended on what could be construed as fawning, and she put a hand to his shoulder. "You're so intelligent when it comes to all these confusing repairs, Eric."

The words, of themselves, seemed sincere. But the lilting note that sugared her voice and her attempt at vamping him, as she'd done his first evening there, only made him frown.

"The day you arrived on our doorstep was surely the most providential day of our lives. I simply don't know what we would have done if—"

He turned to look at her. "Stop."

Instantly, she quit batting her lashes. "Wh–what do you mean?"

He noted the confusion on her face. "Stop trying to be something you're not."

Her eyes widened a little. "I still don't know—"

"You're not Scarlett O'Hara, and you're not your friends. Don't act like those girls, Hannah. You're better than that."

She slowly dropped her hand from his shoulder. "I thought you liked that kind of attention," she all but whispered.

Liked it? He'd only been trying to be polite.

Accustomed to being straightforward, he looked at her intently. "I like you better. The real you. Not these fake interpretations you keep coming up with." He watched her head lower in clear distress. "Why do you keep company with such people, anyway?" he asked more gently. "You're not like them."

Her gaze snapped up. Though the lighting was dim, he sensed a trace of guilt beneath the anger brimming in her eyes. "You have no idea what it's like, having a mother who's half Polynesian, being whispered about and criticized all through childhood, even if she is a chieftain's granddaughter. It didn't matter to them. It made matters worse. The fact that my grandfather is a missionary didn't gain me any favor with my peers, either."

He narrowed his eyes, trying to understand. "You're ashamed of them?"

"No, of course not. I love my mother, and I respect my grandfather for his ideals, though we've never met. But try living among people who judge others for where they come from—and try to fit in despite all that. The boarding school my great-uncle sent me to was full of those kinds of girls. Girls like Muffy and Julia. I was lonely. I wanted friends, just like everybody else had. I soon found I had a gift for literary drama and helped put on school plays. A few of those classmates who would never have anything to do with me before started being kind to me. When the chance came and several of the most popular girls in my class opened their circle to accept me into their fold—two of them from my own hometown—I was determined to do whatever I could to keep their favor."

"Even if that means sacrificing what you believe in?"

She gasped. "What are you talking about?"

"It seems you would have to live a life of pretense in order to keep such friends. Pretending to go along with what they believe while burying your own values, just to be accepted. Life isn't one big stage play, Hannah—it's real, and it hurts, and it can hurt you. You can't go on assuming fantasy roles as an escape just because you're afraid to face who you are."

Flustered, she shook her head. "I'm not afraid—what makes you think I am? Just because I like having a good time and enjoy the motion pictures? Just because I don't look at life as one big depressing newsreel?" She glared at him. "You don't know anything about me."

"I've seen enough."

"All right. Maybe Julia and Muffy can be. . .overbearing. I'll give you that. But at least they offered friendship when others wouldn't give me the time of day!"

"And what kind of friends are they if their primary goal in life is to find new ways to hurt others? I've seen their type, I know what they're like. What makes you think they won't turn on you one day and pull the rug out from under you?"

Her mouth parted in shock, but he continued. "You told me you want my friendship. That's all I'm trying to offer.

I don't want to see you hurt by those girls. Maybe I have no place to talk to you like this. But if you continue hanging around them, I'm afraid you could be hurt very badly. Your schooldays are over, mon amie. It's time you moved on. Are Julia and Muffy really the type of people you want to be with the rest of your life?"

She stood up so suddenly, he felt the rush of air. He looked up at her.

"You're right, Eric. You don't have any place to talk. Especially since you have no idea what you're talking about."

She opened her mouth to say more but instead turned on her heel and marched to her room. The slam of her door told Eric he'd overstepped the line, but he didn't feel sorry about it. He only hoped his well-meaning words had found their mark.

&

Definitely a rogue!

Hannah felt like throwing something.

With her back pressed to her bedroom door, she swung her gaze around the room, looking for a worthy target. Her hand closed around a novel. She hesitated, looking down at the illustrated cover. The memory of his emphatic words twisted in a relentless circle in her mind.

Infuriation, rage, disbelief, mortification, guilt—all fought for predominance. Guilt won.

Tears misted her eyes, and she hung her head.

Earlier, Julia and Muffy had baited Hannah about her pathetic attempts to snag Eric, before he came into the library and put a blissful end to their torment. She had watched his interaction with Muffy and Julia, had mistaken his kind smiles for delight in their interest, and had tried to attract him by emulating her friends. But she'd been wrong. . .so wrong.

He had seen right through her. . .shocked her with his knowing words, angered her with his presumptions of her character, embarrassed her with his blunt disapproval. But more than that, when he looked at her with such concern, admitting his fears to see her hurt, a blade of shame had twisted deep inside her excuse for a heart. The irony didn't escape her, since she was engaging in a plan that could wind up hurting him. Oh, she had hoped in the end it wouldn't, of course, hoped he would laugh it off and chalk it up as a good joke. Or if not that, hoped at least that he might not fall hard for her. But she'd soon discovered Eric wasn't like the boys she'd known. "Boys" in the true sense of the word, immature and insensitive. Silly rich boys who flirted with girls and fell all over themselves to gain their attention. Eric wasn't like that. . .

Eric was a man.

The boys in her social circle cared more about status, wealth, and ego, and less about other people's feelings. Perhaps they deserved to be the target of such a foolish challenge, but Eric did not. Eric put others first and volunteered his help when needed, even when he wasn't shown the appreciation he deserved. He acted more mature than all those boys put together.

"God, what have I done?" Hannah uttered the short plea and set the book down, shaking her head in distress as she moved to her bed. Her novel lay concealed for the moment in her box of photographs of her favorite motion picture stars, but she felt no desire to jump into it and lose herself in the fictional world she'd created.

The world she had control over when nothing went right in her own life.

She stared in dawning shock.

Eric had accused her of crawling within the pages of fantasy to escape life and in the process, lose who she was. Was he right?

She did love to pen her stories but now realized that desire only intensified once she'd gained recognition and acceptance because of her skill, from those who'd shunned her before.

She did have talent, or they wouldn't have been impressed. But maybe she should consider a better way to use her craft, something worthier. She didn't have to give up her stories completely.

An idea teased her mind. Unable to resist the lure, she grabbed pen and paper and jotted everything down, hoping Clemmie would approve. More importantly, hoping Joel would agree. She read through what she'd written, experiencing a sense of satisfaction that had been missing with her unfinished novel. She didn't speculate about the reason too closely, her thoughts finding their way back to Eric.

With grim resolve, she knew what she must do.

And the biggest irony above all ironies. . .

She realized she was falling fast and hard for him.

eleven

The air held a brisk chill, hinting of the weather to come. Eric stood on the green with the rest of the town who'd turned out for the Founder's Day celebration and watched the play unfold. The original plan had been to hold the production inside the colonial-style building, but a broken pipe had made it impossible, flooding the floors of the renovated structure. So the entire affair was being held in front of the building, outdoors.

He stood a short distance from Hannah's family and friends, her brothers giving him hostile glances on occasion. Clemmie had attended with her friend, Thea, their husbands covering the event for the newspaper. Clemmie nodded toward Eric with an uncertain smile, and he sensed her nervousness to have him there.

He hadn't planned to attend but realized how important it was to Hannah that he do so. In the end, he'd agreed, not wanting to injure her feelings. Over the past several weeks, when she wasn't swamped by work on the play or they weren't exchanging clipped words about the value or triviality of their daily lives, he saw a quality in Hannah that intrigued him. Despite everything, she had a sweet naïveté about her, so much different from her haughty friends, and he hoped that gentle part of Hannah would never change.

The play continued, the little colonists and Indians acting out one scene of many in the fictional story Hannah had composed using their town history as a guide. A boy dressed in the clothes of a former century delivered a soliloquy about the founding fathers and their first difficult year, speaking as if he'd also experienced the events by his use of the word *we*, while behind him, other children silently and dramatically acted out the roles of epidemics, crop failures, and more. At times, the boy narrator turned to the side, as if to become part of the audience, and also watched what took place. When that happened, the play became more lifelike as the characters interacted with dialogue, the overall idea unique and interesting. This went on back and forth as the narrator took them through the first hundred years, then solemnly bowed his head. Another narrator, a girl dressed in contemporary clothes, took the opposite side of the stage and continued with the last hundred years of the town's history, also using first person to portray events.

Eric watched, impressed with Hannah's talent to write and organize such a play. He had thought her desire to become a novel writer foolish, in light of all their country suffered, but maybe he'd been too quick to form an opinion. She obviously had creative skills; the play was informative without coming across as heavy or dull.

The only problem that arose she handled smoothly: One of the littlest Indian's feathers came loose from his headband, and he started chasing it over the grounds. The crowd chuckled, as did Eric, and the narrator became flustered, stumbling in his speech. Eric watched Hannah, who stood on the sidelines, quietly say something to the older boy with an encouraging smile, and the narrator resumed while the little Indian chased his feather.

Within minutes of the play's conclusion, Hannah sought Eric out.

"It was awful, wasn't it?"

Her question surprised him, as did her evident insecurity.

"I thought it was good."

"Really?" Surprise lit up her eyes. "You actually liked it?"

He couldn't blame her for her skepticism; he hadn't given her an easy time about how she chose to use her hours each day. "It was very well written."

She smiled then looked uncertain again. "It would have been better with the proper lighting. The spotlights were supposed to be on the narrators at certain moments, for effect, but who could foresee a water pipe bursting?"

"You did the best with what you had and made quick decisions when things went wrong. It was splendid. In fact"—he grinned in sheepish surrender—"maybe such entertainment is good for the soul." Everyone appeared in high spirits, even those in the community he'd rarely seen smile.

She laughed, her features relaxing. "That's high praise, coming from you."

The day continued in a whirlwind of fun, feasting, and laughter. The food was simple fare, but there was so much it practically ran off the tables. Hannah's play and the sight of the provisions made him think of the first Thanksgiving and the nation's celebration of the event, which the president had designated to happen five days from now. Eric noticed Hannah's fixed attention on the food table, her eyes distant.

"Are you hungry?" He captured her attention. "Would you like a sandwich?"

She shook her head. "I was thinking about Shirley and Jimmy."

Her admission astonished him, and he regarded her in tender approval. "Would you like to walk to the park and see if they are there?"

"Oh, could we?" Her eyes sparkled with hope. "I also thought. . .I could locate a box. Maybe we could fill it with food and take it with us?" She sounded hesitant, as if seeking his approval.

He nodded. "I like that idea, *mon amie*. Let's do that."

Once she found a container a little bigger than a shoebox, together they filled it with delicious food until it would contain no more. The hostess behind the table asked their reason for collecting so many sandwiches. When they explained, she told them to wait a moment and disappeared. She returned with a pie and set it on top of the box Eric held.

"For the children." A twinkle lit her eye. "With so much food, it won't be missed."

They thanked her and began their walk to the park. He spotted Julia and Muffy looking at them from across the green, and Eric sensed Hannah go rigid. She grabbed his arm. "Let's go this way. I know a shortcut."

He didn't ask why she wanted to avoid her friends, curious but relieved he wouldn't have to be the victim of the fawning Muffy and the vamping Julia once again.

They strolled through a patch of rough grass, the shrubbery growing closer, clearly not the best of paths to take if it was a path at all. But Hannah's tension soon eased. Her lips turned up at the corners, her eyes bright in her excitement. He had never seen her more beautiful.

Once they reached the area where they'd first met the children, he and Hannah searched but found the park empty. No one was in sight, and he assumed it had to do with the celebration they'd left. He noticed the disappointment cloud her eyes and wanted to make it disappear.

"They said something about an alley behind the coffee shop."

Her eyes brightened again then looked troubled. "Yes, let's try there."

The walk took a short time. The streets were practically empty of traffic. Entering the alley behind the shop, Eric felt Hannah clutch his arm suddenly. "Oh Eric. . ."

Dismay trembled in her voice, and he also felt a wave of horrified sympathy.

Shirley and Jimmy scrounged through a trash bin of rotting garbage like two scrawny alley cats. Another smaller child nibbled from the well-eaten core of an apple turned brown.

"Don't eat that!" Hannah rushed forward.

The curly-haired tot lifted huge dark eyes to them, flashing with fear. The girl dropped the core, whirled away, and ran as if fearful Hannah might lash out and hurt her.

"No—don't go," Hannah called after her. "We brought better food!"

Eric was certain nothing else Hannah could have said would have stopped the panic-stricken child. But at the promise of good food, she cut short her mad retreat and warily turned.

"It's okay," Shirley said. "I know these people, Lily. They won't hurt you."

The girl peered at them distrustfully through her tousled brown curls. Her woolen dress was as dirty as the rest of her, and she wore no coat. Her face was gaunt, her eyes haunted. Eric had become accustomed to seeing such horrible poverty and misery at the mission, especially during the past years of great depression, but he saw Hannah's profound shock at this new slap of reality.

"Why don't you give them the sandwiches?" His voice came as a gentle nudge. He knew from experience that being the one to administer aid would help lift her spirits.

She glanced his way, her eyes glazed with stunned sorrow for the little ones' plight. Gingerly, she took a sandwich in each hand and approached, offering the sandwiches to Shirley and Jimmy. They grabbed the food, bringing it to their mouths in the same motion. The other child, seeing her friends' enthusiastic response, edged closer.

Hannah took another sandwich from the box and, with the same caution the littlest girl displayed, moved forward a few steps then hunched down at a level with the child, smiling and reaching across the small chasm toward her.

"It's really very good," Hannah whispered. "They're from the celebration the town is holding on the green. Did you children not know about that?"

Shirley nodded. "We thought they might throw us out or chase us down if we tried to get some food there."

"Non, it's free to everyone," Eric said when Hannah looked

stricken and unable to speak.

The little girl slowly came forward, her acceptance of the sandwich just as gradual, before taking several quick steps back. Like Shirley and Jimmy, she crammed the bread in her mouth.

"Lily's scared 'cause some people yelled at her and threatened to call the cops last night," Shirley explained. "We sneaked into a snazzy food joint on the other side of town and tried to take food when no one was looking after some people got up to dance. The waiter caught Lily. Me and Jimmy got away. The woman called her filthy and told the waiter to throw her in jail, that the streets weren't safe with vermin like her. She was wearing a sweater like yours."

Eric noticed how the color seemed to rush out of Hannah's face, leaving it white and nowhere near the rose color of her sweater.

"What happened then?" he quietly prodded.

"Me and Jimmy was hiding behind some plants. Jimmy ran and kicked the waiter in the shin so he'd let go of Lily, and I dumped a plate of spaghetti in the woman's lap then grabbed Lily's hand, and we scrammed out of there fast."

"Did your mother know where you were?" Hannah's voice came as a mere wisp, and Eric shot her a concerned glance.

"No, ma'am. She was out looking for work."

"At night?" Hannah's shock didn't escape him.

"Yes, ma'am. She wouldn't have cared." Shirley shrugged. "She don't mind when we find our own meals. Says it's less of a burden on her."

"Is that pie?" Jimmy spoke for the first time, hungrily eyeing the dessert and licking his lips.

"Sure is, son." Eric handed over the box. "Take this home and share it with your little friend. But I want you to make me a promise. No more digging through garbage cans for any of you. Do we have a deal?"

Jimmy shrugged. "I s'ppose."

"You ain't gonna tell on us?" Shirley seemed surprised but relieved.

He wished he had a car to take them home, wished also that his family mission was just down the street. "Who would I tell? Now you three skedaddle before it gets dark. You shouldn't be out on the streets at night."

"Okay—thanks, mister!

"Thanks!" Jimmy echoed his sister as the two took off running. Lily gave them a shy smile before she followed.

Concerned for Hannah, Eric looked at her. "Are you all right?"

"They're so little." Her voice cracked as if it might break. "Too little for this. . ."

Understanding what she didn't say, he put his arm around her shoulders, drawing her to him. Her tight fists lay pressed against his chest. From the manner in which her body trembled, he realized she was trying hard not to cry. It seemed the most natural thing in the world to stroke her hair and bring his other arm around her waist, holding her closer.

After a moment, she lifted eyes shining with unshed tears up to him. The light from the back window of the café made them luminescent. Her lips trembled, and warmth surged through his veins.

He wanted to kiss her.

He might have done just that and had begun lowering his head toward hers, vaguely noting how Hannah's eyes fluttered closed and her chin lifted a little higher, when the back door suddenly swung open, startling them both. Hannah jumped a little in his arms.

At the sight of the cook who scowled at them, she didn't break their embrace but instead nestled against Eric, as if seeking refuge.

"You seen two brats loiterin' around here?" the man demanded.

Eric could feel Hannah bristle with indignation. "It's just us," he said before she could speak and give the children away. The cook had the stub of a cigarette dangling from his mouth, and a dirty apron covered his stout belly. His large, hairy forearms were well muscled, and Eric had a sneaking suspicion that he wouldn't hesitate to strike a child.

The cook gave them a suspicious look, clearly wondering what they were doing in an alley at twilight. Eric stared back gravely, refusing to give an inch.

"Well, then. . ." The man went back through the door. "Guess if them brats are finally gone, it's safe to leave the door open for air so my pies can cool."

Eric felt Hannah tense. "You would let little children starve?"

Eric squeezed her waist in warning. "Don't bother, Hannah." He glared at the man. "Some people you just can't get through to."

"Can't feed the whole world, now can I?" the cook defended, slamming the door—rather than keeping it open as he'd said. Eric wondered if the man thought his pies weren't safe from them.

"It's just so awful." Anger lent a sharp edge to her voice.

"It is," Eric agreed. "But this sort of thing has been going on since the beginning of time. There are always the poor, always the needy, and always those who just don't care." He didn't want to release her but couldn't hold her in the alley all night. "We've done what we could, and three small tummies are going to be satisfied tonight, thanks to you."

His reassurance earned him a grateful smile. Rather than let her go completely, he took hold of her elbow, turning her toward the street.

"Eric?"

"Yes, mon amie?"

"Tell me about your family's mission. I want to know everything."

&

Hannah stood at her bedroom window, looking out at the fresh layer of snow coating the ground. She pulled her sweater closer around her body, then glanced down at its frilled edges. . .a rose sweater of the softest merino wool with pearl buttons. . .a sweater like Julia and Muffy had, when the three bought the same style at a boutique, like sorority sisters. . . a boutique near the boarding school they'd all attended.

The woman called her filthy and told the waiter to throw her in jail, that the streets weren't safe with vermin like her. She was wearing a sweater like yours.

Hannah felt ill. Surely Muffy or Julia wouldn't be so cruel to a starving child? Both her friends had helped with the play and other charity work. . .though both their mothers were on the ladies' committee and perhaps had pressured their daughters into volunteering.

Hannah shook her head to clear it, not wanting to think such ill thoughts. She forced her mind to return to the past week. Giving to those children had brought more pleasure and satisfaction than buying a coveted hat. It had felt more like Thanksgiving to her, sharing Eric's company in an alleyway and bringing smiles to three needy children, than their own small celebration held in the kitchen, since the dining room had been under repairs. Her mother had shared a meal with her father, still bedridden, and Hannah, Eric, and her siblings had eaten their ham around the small table.

It had been pleasant enough—at least Josiah didn't start a fight with Eric, though he barely talked to him. At her mother's insistence, Eric had used their now-working phone to call his family for a distant reunion with his loved ones. But that day couldn't compare to the memory of those moments in the alley. There, for the first time in her young life, she had experienced deep sorrow based in sympathy amid moments that were pure golden.

Golden—in seeing the children's eager response to the offering of food. Golden—in that Eric had held her and almost kissed her.

She should confess the foolish challenge and beg his

forgiveness—had considered it that day—but the opportunity fled forever the moment he took her in his arms.

"I can't tell him now," she whispered miserably. "God, help me. I just can't."

"Yipppeee! Hot dog!"

At the sudden booming hurrah outside her closed door, Hannah nearly jumped out of her skin. She rushed into the corridor, catching David before he could disappear into his room.

"Why did you yell like that?"

"The pond's frozen over! I just heard the news."

All Hannah's worries evaporated with the meaning of his words. She grinned at him before darting downstairs and rushing into the library.

Eric turned suddenly at her abrupt entrance, almost painting a white line across the bottom of the low windowsill. He stared at her in surprise.

"Put your paintbrush down and your tools away. You're coming with me!"

"I need to get this trim finished."

"You don't need to do any such thing, not today. Today is for fun."

He gave her a tolerant smile. "Fun again. I've been having entirely too much of that and not getting enough work done. If I want to make it home before Christmas, I need to concentrate on renovations more and recreation less."

The reminder of his upcoming departure made Hannah falter, but only for a moment. She didn't want to think about that depressing day.

"One more afternoon won't hurt. The pond is frozen over!" She expected some positive response, but he shrugged quizzically. "Ice skating," she clarified.

"I don't know how."

She gaped at him then closed her mouth and shook her head. Why should she be surprised?

"Well, now's the time to learn." She moved his way, grabbing his arm, and did her best to pull him up.

He laughed and allowed her to get him to his feet but shook his head. "I really can't, Hannah—"

"My daughter's right." Her mother walked into the room, smiling and wiping her hands with a dish towel. "I insist that you take some time off, Eric. You've been working too hard, and I'm certain with the little that you told me remains left to do you'll be finished long before Christmas." She smiled. "I even promise I'll not ask you to run more errands or take the children anywhere in the car."

Hannah smiled at her mother, grateful she took her side. He looked from one to the other, his gaze at last settling on Hannah.

"Oh, all right. The painting can wait. But I don't have any skates."

"You can use my husband's. You look to be the same size, and he'll have no need of them this winter."

"Sure he won't mind?" Eric's question came uneasily.

"I've spoken with him in great depth about you. I think he would approve."

Hannah drew a stunned breath, hoping her mother's words went deeper than a pair of ice skates.

Within the next half hour, she and Eric, with David tagging behind, took the car to the pond. David kept quiet, looking at Eric indecisively from time to time, and Hannah hoped he was questioning Josiah's lousy opinion of him.

Soon they pulled into a clearing near the snow-laden trees. Seeing a familiar car, Hannah couldn't help the little squeal that escaped and eagerly looked toward the pond.

❧

"There's Clemmie and Joel!" She waved to a couple across the pond.

Hannah grabbed Eric's hand and pulled him along. He felt amused by her enthusiasm and tense by the cold eyes of the fair-headed young man in whose direction Hannah pulled him. He and Eric were similar in coloring, Eric's hair and eyes a shade darker. When Hannah spoke of her friends, she had joked that Clemmie's husband had been a little imp in behavior, though in looks everyone compared him to an angel when he was a boy; as he grew into a man, the term evolved into warrior angel. The burning look the man gave Eric did remind him of a celestial being who would wield a fiery sword.

"I'm Eric Fontaine." He put out his hand.

The man looked down at it but didn't respond to the gesture. He lifted steady eyes. "I know who you are. I know who your father is, too."

"Joel. . ." His wife slipped her hand around his arm as though trying to restrain him.

"I heard about what he did to you." An icy calm filled Eric. "I'm sorry."

"Sorry?" The man didn't smile. "Your father almost *killed* my wife's mother and on more than one occasion."

"Oh no, not this again! Can we please not talk about this?" Hannah barely suppressed her angry disgust. "I came to enjoy the day, not fight over the past. Anyway, I'm surprised at you, Joel Litton. You weren't exactly guiltless of any of your crimes, yet you found forgiveness. Can't you offer it? Especially—and I don't know how many times I've had to say this—since Eric isn't his father and hasn't done anything wrong! Why must everyone behave so beastly toward him?"

"Hannah, it's all right." Eric squeezed her gloved hand where her fingers still clutched his, her pressure tightening with her words.

"No, it's not. And if this is how it's going to be, then we might as well go find another patch of ice to skate."

She whirled away, but Clemmie hurried forward. "Hannah, wait." She glanced at her husband. A silent message seemed to pass between them before she turned back to Hannah. "You're right. Let's enjoy the day. We rarely have time to spend together anymore. I've been so busy with Rebecca. Mother's watching her this afternoon. Did I tell you she cut another tooth?" She pulled Hannah away as the mood shifted, and arm in arm, both girls began to chatter.

The two men sized each other up.

"The girls are right," Joel said at last. "I shouldn't judge you for your father's sins."

"Since I've come to Cedarbrook, I've learned to get used to it."

"You don't have that problem where you come from?" Joel seemed surprised.

"My father is a changed man. Nothing like the cad of his youth, and I'm sincerely sorry that he endangered you when you were a boy. He told me about those days and meeting you at the carnival."

Joel's eyes narrowed. "Did he? Makes me wonder why."

"He doesn't hide his mistakes or minimize his crimes. In trying to help others find a solution to their problems, he spares himself nothing."

Joel snorted. "How noble."

Eric didn't respond. This man's opinion of his father, the man Joel remembered, was harsh, with good reason.

"I don't want to see Hannah get hurt. She grew up at the Refuge. As well as being my wife's closest and dearest friend, Hannah's like family."

"I would never hurt Hannah. You have my word on that, whatever it's worth to you."

Joel nodded. "Glad we understand each other."

A settlement reached, however shaky, the tension ebbed a few slight degrees.

"Uncle Joel!" a little girl in a bright red coat screeched as she came into view, gliding on her ice skates. "Look at me! Look at me!"

"That's really good, Bethany. You'll be a world champ in no time. Where's your sister?"

The child pointed to the flocked trees behind her, where a

little girl glumly sat on the snow.

"She doesn't want to skate. She's a scaredy-cat."

Joel lifted his brows. "Well then, what do you say we go and help her?"

The girl nodded.

"Your niece?" Eric asked, and Joel looked at him.

"A good friend's daughter. At the Refuge, some developed the habit of calling the adults close to us Aunt or Uncle. Herbert's children do the same with me. He's sick in bed, his wife's busy with their baby, and Clemmie and I offered to take their girls for the day."

Eric nodded, recalling Hannah express that she used the same sort of title for her "Aunt Charleigh" and others there and realized just how close any of them who once lived at Lyons Refuge really were. Like one big family, and clearly protective of each another.

The three moved toward the small, redheaded girl, Eric following only because he spotted Hannah. Both she and Clemmie spoke to the child, who furiously shook her head.

"Don' wanna skate!" she insisted.

Eric quickly took in the situation. Being the eldest of a string of children, his youngest brother four years old, he decided to try and help. "Hi there," he said brightly to the child who sat holding her knees beneath her coat. Tears glistened in her eyes, her expression stubborn.

"I'm a friend of Hannah's. Did you know where I live we don't have a pond like this?"

She didn't respond.

"We have a really wide ocean though. But the water doesn't freeze over like it does here."

She tilted her head to one side, exhibiting a shred of interest.

He looked at the others as though nervous, then hunched down beside her. "Can I tell you a secret? I've never skated before."

Her big hazel eyes regarded him in wonder as if the idea of an adult not being able to partake in the sport was an anomaly. "Are you afraid you might fall down?"

He grinned at her faint words. "Non. Falling down doesn't hurt so much since I've got all this padding." He pulled at the thick sleeve of his coat, noting how well she was bundled up. "I'm afraid I won't be able to get up, and I'll look silly if I try."

She giggled. "Daddy looks like a fish bouncing when he tries."

Eric assumed she meant a fish out of water. "I really would like it if someone would come with me, someone else who doesn't know how, so I won't feel so alone. Would you do that for me?" A return glint of terror in her eyes had him quickly say, "Maybe if your uncle helps you and my friend helps me, we can help one another get up if we fall down. What's your name?"

"Loretta."

"That's a pretty name. So what do you say, Loretta, will you help me not be such a 'fraidy cat?"

A moment's indecision made her scrunch her brow. "Okay."

"Swell." He smiled, sitting down on the snow beside her with the foreign skates. "I'm afraid I don't know how to put these on, either." He pretended to try to pull it over his shoe, and she giggled.

"You're s'pposed to take your shoes off, silly."

"Oh." He gave her a sheepish grin. "Thanks. . .silly." He tweaked her nose, earning him a bigger giggle.

Hannah knelt in the snow to help him while Clemmie helped Loretta rise to her feet. Joel took a few steps his way. "Okay, I'm impressed." His tone came grudging, his smile faint.

"What?" Eric looked up, his expression deadpan. "I meant every word I said."

At that, Joel laughed outright.

Once the strange-feeling shoes with blades for bottoms

were tied successfully to his feet, both Hannah and Joel took his hands and helped him up. Instantly his ankles buckled. "How does one walk in these things?" He stood on snow and was struggling. They expected him to go out on ice?

Amid gales of her laughter, Hannah offered tips as both she and Joel helped Eric.

"Having fun?" he asked dryly when she burst into another fit of giggles while Eric tried to keep his balance on the blades and not walk like a drunkard.

"Okay, I think you're sufficiently practiced," Hannah announced. "Time to get your feet wet on the ice."

Eric grabbed a close, low-lying branch to prevent his fall, showering a mound of snow on his shoes. He gaped at her. "You're joking, *oui*?"

"Non." She grinned. "You've got to get out there some time, *mon ami*. Remember, you have to be an example." Her eyes twinkled too merrily, and he growled in good-natured fun.

"What was I thinking? Maybe that little girl had the right idea all along. . . ."

"Come on, ole sport." Joel clapped him heavily on the back. Had Eric not been holding on to a branch, the action would have brought him to his knees. While relieved that the man had begun to warm to him, Eric questioned Joel's eagerness to get him on the ice. Maybe any friendliness was a sham and Joel looked forward to seeing Eric slam into the freezing hard surface.

Grumbling, he let go of the tree. He held fast to Hannah's hand until he was sure he'd cut off all circulation but somehow managed to plow his way through the snow. He watched as Hannah and Joel glided onto the ice. Joel did a figure eight, and Hannah twirled in a continuous circle.

He stared in disbelief. "They have got to be kidding."

"Just testing it." Hannah smiled at him. "Come on!"

While Joel took Loretta's mittened hand and cautiously helped the child along the ice, a little at a time, with Clemmie holding her other hand, Hannah did her best to support Eric with both arms wrapped around his waist. But her figure was slight compared to his heavier build, and he spent most of his time falling, occasionally bringing her down with him when she couldn't break away fast enough or keep her balance.

As he improved, very slightly, she let him go. But after countless tender landings on his backside, Eric felt thankful they now skated at the edge of the pond, where the blessed bench they'd used stood close in sight.

"Maybe that's enough for one—*agh!*"

His foot slipped out from under him, and he fell backward onto the snow. Hannah reached for him, losing her own balance, and fell frontward—right on top of Eric.

Sprawled atop the length of his body, her laughter quickly ebbed. Their faces close, Eric forgot all about the pain.

They stared into one another's eyes a long moment, their frosty breaths mingling; then his gloved hand went to the back of her head, and he slowly drew her closer.

twelve

Hannah felt his breath, warm against her cool lips, and she clutched his shoulders, her eyes fluttering closed in anticipation of his kiss.

"Smoochin' in the snow! Smoochin' in the snow!"

The teasing shout came from some young boys who ran past, and Hannah's eyes flew open. Eric's hand dropped from the back of her head, but he wasn't looking toward their hecklers. Hannah followed his solemn gaze to the ice, where her brother David had stopped skating and stood, not ten feet away, glaring at them.

Hannah managed to scramble up off Eric, awkwardly but as quickly as she could. She offered her hand to help him up, but he ignored it, somehow managing to get to his feet without falling. "I think I've taken enough bruises and bumps for one lesson." His voice came calm, giving nothing of his feelings away. "How about we take a walk instead?"

Still flustered from being caught by her brother, Hannah nodded at the opportunity to find temporary sanctuary from the others. They stripped off their skates and tugged on their shoes, which Clemmie had stowed in a bag beneath the bench.

"Ahhh. . ." Eric sighed in contentment. "Flat-soled shoes are best."

Hannah giggled, relieved the mood had lightened again. They moved through the woods and along the path near the first few layers of trees that formed a ring, hiding them from the skaters on the pond.

"About what happened. . ."

"That's okay. Forget it. I didn't mind." She felt flustered, certain his quiet words related to their almost-kiss.

"You didn't mind David being angry about seeing us together?"

"Oh, that." Heat rushed to her face at her blunder. "He's barely fourteen. He needs to learn, as does Josiah, who has no good excuse." She barely knew what she was saying. "At least you and Joel seem to have reached an agreement."

"He decided to give me the benefit of the doubt."

"Good." She felt relieved she'd steered him away from her gaffe. "He's really a nice fellow, though you wouldn't believe it to have known him back in the days at the Refuge. And later, when he went blind, he—"

"Joel went blind?" Eric stopped walking. "Not because of anything my father did, I hope?"

"Oh no! It was an automobile accident. Clemmie came to Connecticut and nursed him back to health. Well, emotional health, that is. Joel was an awful curmudgeon then, but Clemmie wouldn't give up on him. Of course, she didn't tell him who she was at first. . ."

She filled him in on what she knew of their story and how Joel realized it was Clemmie he'd loved all along. She gave a wistful little sigh. "It's so romantic."

"It sounds like a novel."

"Or like that movie we saw weeks ago!" Hannah nodded. "Only it wasn't. It all happened. It was very. . .intense."

"Reality is more intense and satisfying than any movie, Hannah."

Something lingered beneath his words, but she was afraid to dig too deeply and find she'd been mistaken. "For someone who doesn't have a lot of experience visiting the motion pictures, you seem rather sure of that."

He chuckled. "It only stands to reason. The motion pictures are just copies of real life."

"But they can be satisfying. That movie we saw inspired me with how she changed toward the end, how she wanted to change. . ."

"I've noticed you've been doing a lot of that lately."

She fairly glowed with his praise. "I do feel different about some issues than before."

A few moments of easy silence passed between them as they walked through the fairy-tale land covered from topmost branch to sloping ground in a thick, fluffy coating of sparkling snow. Beyond the trees, she heard laughter and the happy shouts of skaters.

"Are you still writing your novel?" he asked.

She turned her head to look at him. "You know about that?"

"Abbie might have mentioned it."

She felt herself blushing again, which might have something to do with her hero, who'd taken on the characteristics of the man beside her.

"I dabble now and then. Actually, I've been working on another idea."

"Oh?"

At his clear interest, she wavered. She had hoped to show, not tell him, but then Joel's boss might not agree. "I wrote a piece about Shirley and Jimmy, without mentioning names, of course. A human-interest story, you could call it. But hopefully a method to help—"

He stopped and swung around to face her. "You wrote a piece about those kids?"

She nodded, unable to tell by the sudden softness of his tone matched with the intent look in his eyes if he approved or not. "Joel said he would show it to his boss. I don't know if he'll print it or not. But I tried."

"You're a special lady, mon amie. I think it's a great idea."

"Not so special." Shame made her lower her eyes to his chest when she recalled the silly challenge. She considered telling him and begging him to go along with it, only so that she wouldn't need to purchase two hats with money she didn't have. For her part, when she won, if he agreed to help her, she would tell her friends that they didn't need to pay up. She could never like any hat gained through such a deal. This moment seemed perfect to tell him. But. . .she just couldn't spoil their beautiful outing.

Nor could she bear the look of admiration in his eyes.

"I do a lot of things wrong, Eric. I constantly make mistakes and foolish choices."

"That's all part of being human."

"I'll bet you don't make half as many as I do. You seem so. . . perfect." She spoke the words sincerely, not trying to imitate anyone but herself.

"If you knew what was going through my head right now, you wouldn't say that." His glove lifted to push away her hair that had been blowing in her eyes, and Hannah felt a little thrill go through her.

"What could be so bad to make me change my opinion of you?"

"Not bad. . .just shocking."

"I think I'm intrigued." The words came in a whisper as his eyes lowered to her mouth.

"And I think I would like to kiss you."

Her breath caught on an inaudible gasp, her gaze going to his parted lips. "So, what's stopping you this time?"

At her shy invitation, he cradled her cheek against his hand. His head lowered to hers too slowly, as if he might change his mind, and Hannah did something. . .shocking. At the incredible longing that had been building for days to experience his kiss, she surged up the scant distance left, her mouth firmly meeting his. He let out a gasp of surprise at her eagerness, his warm breath against her lips making her heart pound. She felt her head swim and her hands moved to grab his lapels.

Thankfully, he didn't retreat as she feared he might after her bold gesture. Instead, he brought his free hand to cradle her other cheek while learning her lips with a gentle precision that made her go weak in the knees.

When he did pull away, she opened her eyes and stared at him in bashful wonder. She had written of kisses between the couple in her novel, in complete ignorance. Having experienced her first real one, she realized now she had no idea what she'd been writing about.

His eyes regarded her with tenderness as his thumbs gently stroked her jaw. "It's a good thing we weren't wearing skates."

His light remark alleviated the intense mood, and Hannah giggled. No doubt if they had been in skates, with the way her knees had practically buckled, she and Eric would both be lying in a snowdrift right now.

He looked at her mouth as if he would like to kiss her again, but only dropped his hands from her face. "I think it's time we return to the house. It's getting dark."

Hannah sighed. "I suppose you're right."

They turned to go, and she felt another thrill when Eric slipped his gloved hand inside hers.

❧

The drive to the house was slow due to icy roads, with heavier snow falling. Eric sensed something wrong the moment he opened the door.

The house was too. . .still, but more than that, a strange heaviness weighted the atmosphere. He looked over at Hannah as they removed their coats and scarves. She scanned the room with a frown, and he realized she must sense it, too. David came in behind them and stomped up the stairs without a word. Eric followed Hannah to the entrance of the parlor, where she hesitated, then looked down the corridor. Light flooded the area from the open library door, and she anxiously grabbed his hand and moved that way.

Inside the room, a ladder lay on its side. The floor was covered with loose papers.

"My story!" Hannah rushed forward, dropping to her knees to scoop it up. Eric moved to help.

"No!" Her face flushed with color. "I—I can do it. Thanks."

From an earlier reaction, he had a sneaking suspicion that she didn't want him to see what she'd written.

"But how did the notebook fall all the way from up there. . . ?" Her puzzled gaze went to the highest shelf. A wave of dread washed through Eric.

"Hannah, the ladder."

"What?" She blinked his way.

"Why is the ladder lying on the floor?"

The realization hit them at the same time.

"Abbie!"

"Oh, you don't think. . .surely not. . ." Hannah paled. "She must have climbed it to get my story." With Eric's help, she scrambled to her feet. "She was so angry with me earlier. . ."

Eric groaned. "Me, too. She asked to help, and I told her no. I said she was too little to climb a ladder."

Before they could discover if their fears were true, Esther met them at the door. One look into her frightened eyes made Eric wince.

"Abbie fell off the ladder," Esther confirmed. "Mama caught her trying to get something from the shelf, and she got surprised and fell. Then the ladder fell on her. Hannah, she won't wake up. Her face is so. . .white." The girl's voice trembled.

"Where is she?" Hannah asked fearfully.

"In her room. I have to get more water. Mama's trying to rouse her with cold washcloths."

Her sister ran off. Trembling, Hannah turned into Eric's arms. He held her close.

"If only I hadn't written the stupid thing, if only I didn't always snap at her to leave it alone, to leave me alone. . ." Hannah's tears wet his shirt, and he stroked her hair and back in a gentle effort to soothe. He murmured little meaningless words of consolation, when no words would really ever do. She melted against him, sliding her arms around his waist.

They remained like that for some time, Eric calming her until her body ceased quivering, when suddenly his sleeve snagged at the back of her sweater.

He frowned. "Uh, Hannah. . .we have a small problem."

She moved her head to look at him, an awkward feat when he couldn't move his arm back to let her. "I think my button is caught on your sweater." He could tell the mohair was expensive and didn't wish to wrench his arm away and ruin it. He craned his head to try and evaluate the difficulty. Just as he'd thought, his button seemed to be snagged in the loop of one of the incredibly tiny buttons at the nape of her sweater. Or perhaps in its thread. He couldn't tell—all of it was bright white—and he couldn't tell which button snagged him, either.

"I'm, um"—a rush of heat warmed his face—"going to unbutton the top of your sweater to try to free my wrist." He only wished he could see what he was doing.

She had lowered her head at his first words, and he felt her nod, her face against his chest.

With his free hand, he felt for the top button, managing to slip it from the ridiculously tight elastic loop. His wrist remained caught. He went for the second. Again, nothing. He gave a short nervous cough, wondering how many tiny buttons covered such a small space! Why would any clothing manufacturer put them there? What if it wasn't caught in buttons at all? What if it was caught somehow in the mohair itself? He certainly couldn't undress her!

On the fourth button, he developed a cold sweat.

On the fifth, he was about ready to take off his own shirt and let her remove herself to another room to slip out of the sweater and free his sleeve.

On the sixth, he had a horrible sinking suspicion it wasn't a button his sleeve was caught in.

Just as he was about to suggest another desperate approach, like finding someone who had a clear view and could fix the problem, he heard someone in the corridor.

"What the. . ." Heavy footsteps followed the angry exclamation. Suddenly a hand grabbed the errant sleeve, wrenching it from Hannah's sweater. A button went flying to the floor, but Eric barely saw it before he felt himself swung around and a fist shot toward his mouth. Hannah let out a horrified cry as Eric fell a few steps back with the impact, just managing to stay on his feet. Tasting blood, he wiped it from his mouth.

"Stay away from my sister!" Hannah's older brother glared at Eric and came at him a second time. Eric blocked Josiah's fist before it could slam into his eye.

Hannah sandwiched herself between them. "Josiah—stop! Have you gone crazy?"

"I saw what he was doing, Hannah!" Josiah glared at Eric over her head. "He's a filthy snake, just like his father."

Hannah's entire body shook as she planted her palms on her brother's chest and using all her strength pushed him away from Eric. "He's not! What you saw isn't what you think! His button was caught on my sweater. He was trying to get it free without ripping it—which thanks to you is no longer a possibility."

"He was undressing you, Hannah—I saw!"

"Hardly! The buttons don't go all the way down, and even if they did, Eric is too much of a gentleman to have done that!"

"At the lake, she was lying on top of him." David had appeared at the door, his expression grim. "And he left the ladder in here when he should have taken it back to the shed."

"What?" Josiah's eyes flashed with another burst of rage. Hannah did her best to keep him away from Eric.

"He fell on the ice—I fell on top of him. There's no crime in that! As for Abbie, she shouldn't have been sneaking around in my things. She knows better. I'm the one who pulled Eric away from his work, dragging him from the room, so if anyone's to blame for Abbie being hurt it's me." She glared at her brothers while keeping her restraining palms flat against Josiah's chest. "I am sick to death of the way you both treat Eric. He's not responsible for every evil under the sun as you seem to think! You've both been acting like pigheaded fools, and you should be ashamed."

Eric watched in amazement as she defended him like a growling lioness.

"Your lousy treatment has gone on long enough," she announced. "Our baby sister is upstairs, maybe fighting for her life, and all you two can think about is beating up on Eric and throwing accusations at him? Did you hear me cry for help? Did you see me try and push him away? No. You didn't even ask—you just assumed, again judging him without reason. He's done nothing wrong! And if you can't handle him being in our home, that's just too bad. Because I happen to care about him a great deal, and I want him here, and if you don't like it, well you'll just have to learn to live with it!"

A wave of color washed her cheeks once she blurted the last words. Eric felt shocked by her admission and touched that she'd defended him to her family.

Suddenly, her mother swept into the room. Lines of concern altered her usually placid expression. Her eyes were dark with worry. "What's going on here?"

Hannah told her in a few sentences what had happened.

Her mother looked back and forth between her sons. "I'm ashamed of you. Have I not taught you to keep from jumping to conclusions when you have little of the facts? Your sister is right; your behavior toward Eric has been abominable, and I certainly wouldn't blame him if he left us tomorrow. He's been a godsend to us. You've misjudged him, and it will stop now. There are more urgent matters that need to be addressed. I cannot reach the doctor."

Eric remembered meeting the man at the Founder's Day

celebration and also recalled where he'd last seen him. "He's at the pond. I can take the car and tell him."

She shook her head. "No, the roads are too icy. Our neighbor has a sleigh. I will call to ask. A sleigh will be faster."

"I'll go with you." Hannah moved with Eric into the foyer, and they grabbed their coats.

Josiah suddenly appeared, tense but not looking ready to throw another punch. He addressed Eric. "You know how to rig a sleigh?"

"With Hannah's help, I can manage."

"She doesn't know how, either. I'll do it. We had one at my great-uncle's."

With that, the young man left, again surprising Eric, who'd been sure he would demand his sister stay behind. He shrugged into his coat, still cold from their earlier outing.

"They'll come around," Hannah reassured, grabbing her outerwear, "especially with Mother on your side."

"Don't worry about me," he soothed, helping her into her coat. "I'm a big boy. I can handle it."

She faced him suddenly, her fingers lifting to the corner of his mouth and taking him by surprise. "Does it hurt?"

"I have brothers, too, and we didn't always get along. A punch in the mouth is nothing." He smiled to reassure her. "Let's go find help for your little sister."

The concern deepened in her eyes, and he slipped his hand around her sleeve in consolation as they hurried to the neighbor's.

thirteen

On any other occasion, Hannah would have been thrilled with such an outing. The sleigh rides to the pond and back on a clear, moonlit night, while sitting nestled up against Eric, composed the essence of romance. The neighbor's two grays dashed over the ground, pulling the sleigh in a swift, crisp slice through the drifts of snow. Yet Hannah could think only of her baby sister, and she clutched Eric's hand under the blanket, grateful for his strength.

"When I said you should face reality, I never wanted you to suffer anything like this." His voice came quiet, and she squeezed his glove.

"I know. And don't apologize. You were only trying to shake me out of my dreams to see the real world."

He frowned as if unhappy with her reply. "There's nothing wrong with dreams, Hannah. Keep them. A little entertainment is good for the soul, too."

At his admission, she laid her head against his shoulder, not daring to tell him that he was good for her soul. Since he'd arrived in Cedarbrook, she'd been intrigued by him, drawn to him, enamored of him. . .and now, she knew without a doubt, in love with him. She loved Eric, and despite the current tragedy, she felt a new peace with him she'd never experienced. A sweet. . .serenity. Something she'd never known she was missing until she found it with him. He accepted her, faults and all, and didn't wish her to be anyone else.

But he doesn't know about the challenge yet, Hannah.

Her conscience nagged at her, but she closed her eyes to the thought. Now was not the time. Later. . .

Much later, after they'd arrived home and the doctor had departed once he'd seen Abbie, the family gathered in the parlor.

"Besides a broken arm, which the doctor has set," Hannah's mother informed her worried children, "Abbie took a nasty bump to the head. The doctor said if she doesn't awaken by morning, it could be bad. She mustn't be moved. Now, I must see to your father."

Hannah moved forward. "Is there anything I can do to help, Mama?"

Her mother's harried expression gentled. "Pray, my daughter. All of you children, pray." She swept out of the room.

"Yes, we all will. Won't we?" Hannah looked at her brothers. They drew closer. Hannah slipped her hand into Eric's and felt relieved when Esther took his other one. At least she'd never shown him animosity. David took Hannah's other hand, Josiah took Esther and David's, all of them forming a circle.

"Eric, you're probably better at this than we are." Hannah felt ashamed to admit that, remorseful of just how far she had slipped in her faith since living at her great-uncle's. "If you wouldn't mind?"

He dipped his head in a nod, bowed it, then offered up the most touching and heartfelt prayer for Abbie's full recovery, the doctor's wisdom, and her family's peace. Hannah stared at him in wonder. Afterward her brothers exchanged glances; then Josiah looked at Eric.

"Listen, maybe I had you figured all wrong. When I heard about the reign of terror your father caused, then seeing you with my sister and knowing you were living here, well, maybe I jumped the gun like Mother said."

"Yeah, me, too," David admitted, his grin sheepish.

"That's all right." Eric smiled and stuck out his hand in a peace offering. "I have sisters, too, and if I ever thought any man might hurt one of them. . .well, I probably would have done the same thing." Both boys took turns shaking his hand.

Josiah grinned. "How's the jaw?"

Eric rubbed his hand along the offended part of his face. "You throw a mean punch."

"I boxed one year in high school."

"It shows."

Hannah knew that was the closest her brothers would probably ever come to an apology. But Eric's response astounded her, and she felt he was being too kind. She shook her head in amazement as she watched the fellows exchange pleasantries and thanked God for small miracles.

The doorbell rang.

"I'll get that," Hannah said, but they were too deep in discussion on the subject of the economy to hear her. She glanced at her sister who'd started to pick up the papers Hannah had abandoned, looking at each. "Esther! You get the door—I'll pick those up."

She snatched the papers from her sister's hand, and Esther took off running as Hannah scooped up as much of her manuscript as she could and shoved it in the notebook. The story wasn't sinful, but it didn't make her proud, and she almost wished she'd never started it. Maybe if she hadn't been so secretive about the whole thing, Abbie wouldn't have fallen.

"Hannah?"

An uncertain yet awed element in Esther's voice brought instant alarm. Hannah noticed the fellows had stopped talking, too. They all turned toward the entrance.

An older gentleman with a solid, wiry build, his face bronzed and weathered by years as if he spent a great deal of time outdoors, came in behind a wide-eyed Esther. His hair shone gray, his eyes shimmered bright green, and Hannah realized with a curious start they were full of tears.

"Hello," she said uneasily. "May we help you?"

He smiled, and she sucked in a breath, knowing she'd seen that smile before.

"Papa!" Hannah heard the shriek and watched in wonder as her usually sedate mother ran down the stairs and toward the man. She vaulted into his arms, throwing hers around his neck. He returned her embrace with just as much gusto as tears streamed down both their faces.

"Oh Papa—you didn't say you were coming! Oh Papa, you came at just the right time. I don't know what to do."

"There, there, my little Sarah. Papa's here. It's all right. . . there, there. . ."

Hannah blinked in shock as she watched her mother fall apart in the arms of her father, whom her mother hadn't seen since she left the island when she'd gotten married.

Eric came up beside her and offered her his handkerchief. It was then Hannah realized she was also crying. She noticed her siblings gape at the emotional display. Sensing the newly reunited father and daughter needed time alone, Hannah motioned that they should all leave.

They walked past her grandfather, still holding and comforting her mother, and Hannah pulled Eric with her into the kitchen. "I never even considered all she must be going through. First Daddy, now Abbie. And I certainly never gave her an easy time of things. I just never thought. . . she's always been so strong, the rock in our family."

Seeing her mother in such a distressed state shocked Hannah more than she let on, and she couldn't stop trembling.

"Even the strongest rocks chip from time to time," Eric soothed, rubbing his hands up and down her arms as if to warm her. "Your mother will be all right. Especially now."

"I just never realized how hard it's been for her. I've had my eyes closed to a lot of things, too involved in my own little world. Well, they're open now." Her eyes widened, as if in emphasis to her words. "And my *grandfather* has come. I never thought I'd get to meet him. Now if only Abbie would recover."

"I think it's a good sign that your grandfather arrived when he did. Maybe it's God's way of offering hope."

Hannah nodded, moving into Eric's arms and resting her head against the sure, steady beating of his heart. Oh, how she loved this man! And how she had wronged him. He had easily forgiven her brothers. Could he forgive her if she told him what she'd done?

She lifted her head to look into his eyes, but again all thoughts of confessions scattered—this time when he tilted her chin farther upward and delivered the softest of kisses to her lips. Sweet warmth melted through her, and the gentlest of sighs winged through her heart as she returned his tender affection.

The door suddenly slammed open. They jumped apart in shock, looking toward the entrance.

Esther stood there, her face beaming. "Abbie's awake! And the first thing she asked was if she could now be waited on like Daddy!" She giggled. "Daddy even used a cane to go into her room, and Mama's there, too. And our grandfather!" Her eyes grew brighter. "Abbie's okay, and our grandfather's come to meet us! Oh Hannah. Isn't life grand?"

"Yes, it is, Esther. Absolutely splendid." Hannah laughed in tearful relief and smiled at Eric. "It feels as if Christmas has visited us early this year."

❧

"My daughter tells me your family runs a mission. I'd like to hear more."

Eric looked up at Mrs. Thomas's father from across the table where the two men enjoyed sandwiches and coffee. Ever since Josiah LaRue arrived three days ago, he and Eric had bonded, spending hours in discussion. The former missionary had been the anchor his family needed, and Eric admired the man for the lifetime he'd devoted to his calling.

Eric filled him in on all his family had done to help their community, even broaching his own fledgling idea.

Mr. LaRue's eyes widened in appreciation. "That sounds like a worthy cause. I'd like to be part of it if you decide to do it. Mission work runs in my blood. Even though I retired and left the island to be with my family again, I don't want to quit the field completely."

Eric smiled. "I'd be honored for you to help us, sir."

The man looked at the clock and stood from the table. "My brother should be home from his trip, and I think it's time we made amends. He never did like that I chose missionary work. But he did for Sarah and her family what he could, and I must thank him for that, among other things." The man chuckled, shaking his head in wonder. "You can imagine my surprise when I found out by a fluke that my brother was the anonymous donor who'd been supporting my work for years by paying for all necessary supplies to be shipped to the island. Somewhere in that stony heart of his, I believe there might be some good soil and a sprout in need of watering."

He chuckled, and Eric grinned as he walked with the man to the foyer. He turned as he opened the door. "We'll talk more about your idea later."

"I'd like that—" Eric abruptly ended his sentence when he noticed Hannah's newly arrived visitor.

"Hello, Julia." The informal greeting seemed wrong, somehow, too personal when he didn't want that at all. But he didn't know her last name.

"Hello, Eric." Her smile seemed seducing.

Hannah's grandfather, whom she completely ignored, looked from the woman to Eric, his eyes issuing a warning. *Watch out, son, this one's trouble.*

Eric nodded. He didn't need to be told twice.

Once Hannah's grandfather left, Eric tried to play the polite host and opened the door for her to enter. "Hannah's upstairs with her sister. I'll tell her you're here."

"Oh, that's not necessary." She grabbed his sleeve before

he could leave. "I came to inquire about Abbie." Her features softened in concern, and Eric wondered if he'd misread her. She seemed to care about the little tyke. And he knew the pain of being judged for a crime not committed.

"Abbie's improving every day. She's demanding and fussy, and I understand those are her usual traits, so I'm sure she'll be fine."

Julia laughed. For a moment the mask seemed to break as her coolly collected features showed a flash of warmth. "That's wonderful." She seemed suddenly uncertain. "Might we talk? Somewhere more private?"

Eric narrowed his eyes in suspicion, wondering what she was up to.

"Please. I need to talk to someone, and you seem so nice. Like the type who really cares about people."

He didn't bother asking why she didn't confide in her own friends; her last comment explained that. Still uneasy, he motioned to the parlor door. "We can talk in there."

"Yes, please. Thank you."

Her sudden switch to meek behavior took him aback. He allowed her to precede him into the finished room, now warmer and brighter with new flowered paper covering the walls.

"I have a confession to make," she began softly.

He nodded for her to go on, wondering what she'd done to cause him harm.

"I didn't want to do it, but Hannah insisted."

fourteen

Against the pillows that supported her, Abbie bowed her bandaged head in shame. "I'm really sorry I tried to take your story, Hannah. I won't do it again."

Hannah, grateful her sister was alive and well, felt she could forgive anything. "And I'm sorry I treated you badly when we first moved here and at Uncle's, too. You're so important to me, Abbie." Carefully, she leaned forward and embraced her baby sister, who wrapped her one good arm around Hannah's back. Abbie's other arm hung encased in plaster in a sling about her neck. The poor girl looked like a war orphan, and Hannah kissed her forehead beneath the white bandage, then the tip of her nose, cradling her small chin with her fingers to look her in the eye.

"No more climbing ladders, though."

Abbie sighed. "Yes, I know. But no one ever lets me do *anything*. You say I'm just a baby, but I'm not."

"Hmm. I see now how that's upset you. And it takes a really big girl not to cry when I know how it must hurt. So, you get better, and we'll see about changing that old rule. Deal?"

Abbie grinned. "Deal!"

"Good. Get some rest now." Hannah moved away. She never made it out the door.

"Can you bring more hot cocoa? And cookies?"

Hannah affected a stern countenance. "Any more sweets, and you'll be dealing with a tummy ache, too."

"Please, Hannah," her sister cajoled. "I'm still hungry."

"Well. . ." She smiled, knowing she would surrender in the end. These past three days, Abbie had reigned supreme as a little princess in the Thomas home, no one able to refuse her anything. "All right, but don't say I didn't warn you."

At the bottom of the staircase, Hannah heard voices in the parlor. Curious, she moved to the open doorway, shocked when she saw Eric offer Julia his handkerchief, and she dabbed at her eyes with it.

"Thank you, Eric. You don't know what a relief it is to get that burden off my chest. Hannah should never have done such a horrid thing. I thought you should be warned, since I don't want to see you hurt. You're so sweet, any girl would be lucky to have you, and Hannah was wrong to treat you so callously."

In gaping shock, Hannah watched Julia slip her hand behind Eric's neck and move up to kiss him. He averted his face at the last moment and stepped back, causing her lips to brush his jawline instead.

Hannah moved forward, hurt and angry, the truth a harsh slap in the face.

They turned at her entrance. Julia's face paled, but her eyes sparked in triumph. "It's over, Hannah. I told him. I just could no longer take part in your cruel little scheme."

"Is it true?"

Eric's low, quiet voice broke through Hannah's rage. She swung her gaze to his, her anger fading as she looked at him, her eyes going wide and anxious.

He knows. . . . Dear God, help me. He knows.

"Yes," she said simply, weary of the deception and realizing she deserved every bit of his censure.

"You wanted to make me fall madly in love with you?" His brows drew together in curiosity as he moved toward her. "Why?"

She swallowed hard, nervous by his slow advance, unable to admit her reprehensible part in the foolish challenge and her desire to prevent any wounded pride. She realized she'd been as shallow and selfish as Julia and dropped her eyes in shame.

He stopped before her while she waited for the hammer to drop. Gently he tilted her chin up to force her wary eyes to meet his serious blue ones.

"When falling in love with you was the easiest thing to do, *ma chère*," he continued, then dropped a kiss to Hannah's parted lips that left no doubt he meant what he said.

Stunned by the turn of events, she felt her knees buckle and clasped his arms tightly, barely hearing Julia's huff of disgust as her former friend whisked from the room. The slam of the front door hardly registered, as incredible warmth rushed through Hannah. Eric deepened the kiss with a small groan, as though he couldn't help himself, and cradled her head in his hands. Her heart pounded harder. For the first time, she wished for the old chill of the parlor in the now uncomfortably hot room.

He abruptly pulled away, his breathing as uneven as hers, and looked into her eyes as if to gauge her thoughts. She saw the hurt there and sensed his mood change.

"Did you mean it?" she whispered.

"Did you?"

She knew what he referred to and that no way existed to make it sound less awful than it was. She lowered her hands from his shoulders where they had slid. "I felt cornered into Julia's challenge. She instigated it, not me. I didn't want to be thought of as juvenile. I really did like you from the start, and I hoped you would see it as a harmless prank." She swallowed, nervous. "Then I began to care about you more, about hurting you, and I realized how juvenile I'd really been. But I didn't see a way out of it. The more time we spent together, the worse I felt. I never meant to hurt you, Eric, and I never should have agreed to that silly challenge."

"No, you shouldn't have." She lowered her chin in distress, and again he lifted it, his eyes gentle. "But I forgive you."

She blinked. "How? I mean. . ." She struggled for words. "I hoped you would—I'd planned to tell you sooner. And

I'm relieved, you have no idea how much! But how can you always so quickly forgive, no matter how badly you've been hurt?"

He smiled wryly. "I've had a lifetime of lessons. After hearing my father's testimony on a continual basis and understanding the terror he inflicted on so many—especially your own family—I can hardly hold grudges, Hannah. Your aunts, despite any lingering fear they might still possess, *did* forgive my father, and he never forgot that. It's what helped lead him on the road to salvation, and he instilled that lesson of forgiveness into all his children. Life is too short to hold animosity against anyone. We all make mistakes, ma chère. I've made them, too."

Her heart full by his quiet admission and her newest feelings for him, she whispered, "I truly do love you, Eric." Her eyes widened when she realized she'd spoken her thoughts, but he only smiled.

"Enough to marry me, *mon amour*?"

"Wha—" Sure she'd heard wrong, her legs grew unstable again, and she grabbed his arms a second time.

"Maybe we should sit down."

She nodded, and he helped her to the sofa, taking a seat beside her.

"I've spoken with your grandfather and still need to discuss it with my parents. But I have an idea and want you to be part of it. Actually, you gave me the idea when you mentioned you wished your town had a mission. I want to start one here for people like Shirley and Jimmy and Lily to come and get at least one hot meal a day. A place where they can hear about Jesus' love, a place that can offer help to families and perhaps even find them work."

She tried to follow his eager news, her brain still whirling with his former question. "That sounds wonderful—but. . . did you just ask me to marry you?"

He grinned. "Oui. I've been wanting to for a while. Maybe

I should have waited until your father was at least tolerant of the idea of me for a son-in-law, but I couldn't hold back any longer. I'm sorry if it wasn't very romantic."

Not romantic? Any more romance, and he would have had to fetch the smelling salts. She shook her head in wonder. "Despite all I've done, how selfish I've been, you want me for your wife?" The words seemed incredible; she could scarcely believe them.

"Like I said, everyone makes mistakes. That's not who you are. I've watched you since I've been here. You've changed, mon amour. I've watched you evolve, like a butterfly breaking out of a cocoon. I said so earlier, and I'll say it again—loving you was the easiest thing to do."

His poetic words and French endearments warmed her heart; she could listen to them forever. "Yes, I'll marry you, Eric." After another breathless kiss that made her grateful for the sofa now supporting her legs, she softly breathed, "When?"

"Whenever you'd like."

"I've always wanted a Christmas wedding."

His eyes flared a bit in surprise. "That's only a few weeks away. Don't you have to prepare and get things ready and do whatever it is you women do?"

She laughed. "Right now I don't care if we get married by a justice of the peace. I just want to be your wife as soon as I can and live out our dream together!"

Elated, she kissed him again. Certain nothing could burst her bubble of joy, she then grabbed his hand and pulled him with her out of the parlor. "Let's tell Mother and Daddy now. I can't wait another second!"

❧

"No—absolutely not!"

"Bill. . ." Mrs. Thomas put a hand to her husband's shoulder as he bolted upright in bed.

Eric remained somber, not surprised. He felt Hannah's hand tighten around his.

"Daddy!" she insisted, "You're not being fair. Mama's told you what a wonderful man Eric is, and so has Grandfather. Can't you take their word for it if you can't take mine?"

The expression in his eyes softened as he turned toward his daughter. "This has nothing to do with Eric's character. I'll admit, I was wrong about him. After these last months of having him in our home and hearing your mother's praises of him every single day, I realized there must be some good there for my Sarah to think so highly of him."

Hannah shook her head in confusion. "Then what. . . ?"

"You're too young. You're seventeen, and you're what?" He looked at Eric. "Eighteen?"

Eric gave a swift nod. "Nineteen in January, sir."

"That's just too young."

"Mama was barely seventeen when she married you," Hannah argued, a hurt tone to her voice, "and Clemmie was only a little over my age when she married Joel."

"They were more mature. They both faced struggles in their young lives, which made them mature far past their years. You've had life handed to you on a silver platter for so long and are just learning how to deal with adult issues."

"I may be young, but at least I never judged Eric falsely like so many in this household did. At least I gave him the benefit of the doubt and trusted him. Something you never did."

Eric squeezed her hand in both comfort and warning. But the angry tears in her eyes showed she wouldn't be stopped.

"You lied to me, Daddy. Why? You never said you were a gangster and that was why you were the target of that awful man who shot Mama and killed my unborn sister or brother. You've taught us to be honest. But the truth is you really don't like Eric any more than before, isn't that right?"

"Hannah!" her mother reprimanded sharply, and Hannah lowered her eyes.

"Did you tell her?" Her father's eyes snapped to Eric's.

"He assumed I knew already. It wasn't his fault. You

shouldn't have hidden the truth from me, Daddy."

"Perhaps we should wait to speak of this when we've all calmed down," her mother suggested quietly.

Hannah's father patted her mother's hand resting on his shoulder. Looking to Eric, then Hannah again, he spoke. "No. Now that she knows that much, she should know the rest."

They shared a grave look, and her mother nodded.

"I didn't tell you about my time as a gangster for two reasons, Hannah. I kept it hidden, not wanting it to affect your life—not wanting your friends to somehow learn and give you grief, making you an outcast among them. We had decided to leave New York and the Refuge after Eric's father sent us a message, warning us of danger. The Piccoli bunch found us before we could, and well, you know what happened after that." He closed his eyes a moment in remembered pain. "When you were little, we learned your mother's uncle was alive and living in Connecticut, and we took the opportunity to put New York behind us for good. Those men I worked for are ruthless, honey. Every day, I regret joining up with their organization. But that doesn't change the fact that I did."

Hannah gasped. "That's why you never allowed me to go to New York City, isn't it?"

"That's part of it. Years have passed with no sign of trouble, but you can never be too careful. When Eric arrived, it felt like the old dangers had resurfaced, since his father was my associate. That's one reason I treated you so badly." He met Eric's eyes. "I'm sorry, son."

Eric nodded, too stunned by the man's confession to respond. Hannah released his hand and hurried to embrace her father. "I'm sorry, too, Daddy. I've been so angry with you ever since I found out. I should have just come straight out and told you that I knew. I understand now."

Her father smoothed her hair. "Unless you've lived through such an ordeal, you can't begin to know the fear, Hannah.

I almost lost your mother. I did lose our child. God forgave me, but it took a long time before I could forgive myself. And I couldn't bear for you to look at me with hatred, knowing all I'd done."

"Oh Daddy, I could never hate you."

They embraced again, and Eric felt he also understood much more than before. That her father would speak so freely in front of him showed Eric something else: He had won his trust.

"I never said you two couldn't get married." Her father brought the subject back around to them. "Just that you wait. One year. You two have known each other such a short time. It's too soon to talk of marriage. If the love is there, if this is what God wants for you, then nothing will prevent it from happening." He reached for his wife's hand, and she shared a tender look with him, forged through long years of shared devotion, tragedy, and trust. One day Eric hoped to share such a look with Hannah.

"Your father's right," Eric spoke, earning him a grateful look from her parents. "I know my feelings for you are true, Hannah, but it's best to wait. There's much I need to accomplish, and this way you'll get your dream wedding." He smiled. "You can't tell me you don't still wish for one, knowing you as I do."

Her face aglow, she rose from her father's side and approached Eric. "I promise you this, Eric Fontaine Jr. In one year's time, I'll be walking toward you in our church on the green to become your bride."

"I love you, Hannah. That won't change. I'll wait for you forever if I have to."

She slipped her arms around his waist, tilting her head back, her smile warming him. He glanced toward her parents, grateful to note they didn't seem displeased by their daughter's public affection. Likewise, he slipped his arm around her back.

"I've already told Hannah. I want to make Cedarbrook my home, to start a mission here. I like the peacefulness of your small town, and I like what it has to offer." At this, he again looked at Hannah and smiled. "The best in all of Connecticut."

fifteen

A little over one year to the day, Hannah stood in the back of the church, ready to take her first steps down the aisle and become Eric's wife.

She smiled at her sisters, who carefully smoothed the satin folds of her gown, and also at Muffy, her bridesmaid, who straightened the veil Hannah's mother had attached to her upswept hair. Muffy had grown weary of Julia's cattiness and cruel games and appeared one day to volunteer at the new mission Eric and Hannah's grandfather ran. At first Hannah had been wary, remembering her friend's designs on Eric, which Muffy later apologized for. It also came as a relief to learn Muffy hadn't been the woman diner in the rose sweater to hurt Lily—evident when the child shyly offered her hand and smiled upon meeting Muffy. Clearly it had been Julia, which came as no shock. Like Hannah, Muffy had been raised in wealth, but insecure in her own skin, she fed off people like Julia for reassurance. Muffy and her family had become one of the mission's strongest supporters, and Clemmie, Hannah, and Muffy had become fast friends.

Throughout the past year, Hannah and Eric wrote to one another constantly, and he visited often to oversee the building of the mission and to see Hannah. She'd been shocked to learn that Eric came from old money on his mother's side. His father was also wealthy, though their family lived modestly. Eric Sr. used his ill-gotten gains long-ago stolen from his nameless victims to help the needy, and a good chunk of his inheritance as comte he'd put aside for his grandchildren. Eric Jr. had been supportive of Hannah's journalistic efforts, which Joel also encouraged, the human-interest stories she wrote gaining recognition for the mission. She'd never abandoned her novel entirely, even adding to it to make it more inspiring, but it was no longer her focus. Fame wasn't her goal.

Her goal waited at the end of the aisle.

Their love had grown, ever changing, into something rich and indefinable. In the past year, Hannah had matured in her quest to help the needy, now grateful her father had made them wait to marry. She'd been such a child, too foolish and silly to take on the role of Eric's wife. But now. . .now she was ready to take on all of what that entailed.

Hannah felt a momentary unease at the thought of how her entire family would react to having Eric's father in their presence once again. Her brothers and friends had at last accepted her fiancé, and now Eric and Joel were good pals. She'd even heard her brothers ask Eric for advice, and Hannah's heart warmed every time she heard her father call him *son*.

But she knew old grievances, especially those Eric Sr. had caused, could bring lasting bitterness. Everyone had struggled to accept Eric Jr., who'd done nothing wrong, judging him by his father's many sins.

And now his father was present among them.

Long ago, Aunt Charleigh and Aunt Darcy had forgiven him, then walked away, never expecting to see him again. Could they—her entire family—accept Eric's father as part of their family?

She'd met him the previous evening at their hotel room, a little awed, nervous, and fearful to approach despite knowing that he'd changed. Nevertheless, the old horror stories of all he'd done whirled within her mind as the tall and slender, leonine man—her soon to be father-in-law—stood to greet her. He bowed over her hand with a charm that must have won many in his cons. She gasped a faint greeting, vaguely noting where her fiancé had received his heart-stopping, attractive looks, indeed his whole manner.

Eric Sr.'s dark blue eyes twinkled with reassurance and

kindness, nothing dangerous or frightening in their depths. "Don't worry. I don't bite," he greeted her lightly with the faint lilt of a French accent, instantly setting her at ease. "Ma chère, it is a pleasure to welcome you into my family. To finally meet the woman whom my son speaks of day and night—"

"Father. . ." Eric Jr. fidgeted in embarrassment but grinned at Hannah.

She had smiled as Eric's father kissed her hand. She then surprised them all by moving forward to kiss his cheeks, as she knew the French did from the movies she'd seen. "Merci, I'm happy to meet you at last. Your son speaks highly of you and your work at the mission."

"Then I think I enjoyed the better of the conversations," his father said with a wink.

Eric's mother, Janine, a lovely brunette, was sweet and gentle, greeting Hannah with a warm hug. It was clear she doted on her husband, often touching his arm or hand, and Eric's nine siblings clearly loved their father.

"It's time. Are you ready?" Clemmie squeezed Hannah's arm, bringing her to the present. Hannah had insisted that Clemmie be her matron of honor, dispensing with the idea of a maid of honor.

"Oh yes. As you once said on your wedding day—I think I've been ready forever."

The girls softly chuckled, and Clemmie left to join the bridesmaids at the front of the sanctuary. Smiling, Hannah took her father's arm, prepared to take the first step into her new future.

The church, decorated with white satin ribbons and matching roses, was indeed lovely, but Hannah only had eyes for Eric. He looked handsome in his tuxedo, and she inhaled a swift breath to realize that their day had really arrived.

"I love you, kitten," her father whispered before they began the march down the aisle as the music played. "I hope you'll be very happy together."

"I love you, too, Daddy. And I know we will be, just like you and Mama."

Within minutes, she exchanged vows with Eric, reverently, the moments passing as if in a dream, a fantasy.

But this was better than any novel or motion picture ever made.

A reformed princess and a missionary vicomte. . .

A benevolent handyman and an amateur writer. . .

Soon to embark on their own life story.

Once the final blessing was given, Eric's lips touched hers, and Hannah laid her hand against his cheek, leaning into the warmth of his kiss.

Oh yes, much better. . .

The best reality had to give.

❧

The sweet feel of Hannah's lips against his made every long, excruciating day Eric had spent without her this past year dissolve. He almost forgot where they were, but at Joel's amused clearing of his throat, Eric remembered and managed to let her go. For now.

"Plenty of time for that later," his best man said low enough that only Eric could hear. He had learned of his friend's partiality for mischief and ignored him, taking Hannah's arm.

"Shall we, Mrs. Fontaine?"

Her eyes sparkled in delighted wonder. "Gladly, my husband."

They smiled at each other, then hurried to exit the church, many of the guests already waiting to shower them with rice. Squealing, Hannah grabbed his arm as they tried to duck the showers of grain thrown their way.

A short time later, Eric and Hannah arrived at Great-Uncle Bernard's manor for the reception, both of them anxious about how Eric's father would be received.

Hannah's great-uncle had mellowed, according to Hannah. Similar in looks to her grandfather, his skin sallow instead of bronzed and weathered, her great-uncle was a congenial host and offered them his best wishes, happily receiving Hannah's fervent hug. Ever since the two brothers had reunited, they'd been close. Her parents and great-uncle had also mended their differences, and shortly afterward Hannah's grandfather had brought his older brother to Christ. Hannah's great-uncle had become a staunch supporter of the mission, and with so much capital, Eric now hoped to build a bigger shelter where the homeless could not only enjoy a hot meal and hear of God's love, but also have a bed and find rooms devoted to entire families. It was a dream for the future, but he'd learned that God did make dreams come true.

The reception was held in the grand hall, the curtains of the wide window drawn for a breathtaking view of the softly falling snow and the white-coated wood beyond. White roses garnished with satin ribbons decorated the area, and friends and family filled the room.

Shirley and Jimmy giggled nearby, sneaking swipes of frosting from the bottom of a seven-tiered cake. Their mother, working as a maid for Hannah's great-uncle, lightly slapped their wandering hands and told them to behave.

Catching sight of Hannah and Eric, the children immediately ran to them as they always did at the mission. Hannah didn't seem to mind that Jimmy crumpled the satin bows on her gown, laughing in delight as she reached down and returned his exuberant hug.

"You're pretty," Jimmy said with awe, staring at Hannah.

Eric pushed a lock of tousled hair from the boy's eyes. "Hands off, son. She's mine," he teasingly warned, earning him a big smile from the little boy. Both children glowed with vitality and health.

"Where's Lily?"

Their small friend never tagged far behind. Shirley pointed, and Eric was amazed to see Lily half sitting and half standing on his father's lap, excitedly chattering to him. The five-year-old had come a long way from the frightened little scarecrow he'd once met scrounging for food in an alley. Hannah's great-uncle had also hired Lily's mother, in fact, giving jobs whether in his home or his offices to whomever Hannah and Eric presented to him.

But while Lily had clearly accepted his father as her friend, Eric noticed Hannah's family and friends had not. They remained on the opposite side of the room, casting his father wary glances at best, hostile ones at worst. At least the children from both families seemed to play well together. Eric hoped that as the evening progressed and the gaiety multiplied, their parents' hesitation would decrease.

He hoped in vain.

"Is everything all right, darling?"

Hannah came up beside him, slipping her hand into his, her endearment touching his heart. He lifted her hand to his lips for a brief kiss. "Our plan to bring the families together is at a standstill, mon amour."

Hannah's brow creased with concern. "Should I talk to them?"

Mr. LaRue approached, fiercely hugging his granddaughter and offering Eric the heartiest of congratulations. "What's this?" Hannah's grandfather held her by the shoulders, peering closely at her. "Is that sadness I see in those beautiful eyes? What's wrong, my girl?"

Hannah grimly told him the situation.

"Is that so?" He looked her family's way, then smiled thinly in determination. "This is your wedding day, and I know how long you've both waited for it. You should be enjoying it, not worrying about other people's foolishness. Let's see what your old grandfather can do to help."

Eric had never admired the man more than when he watched him walk across the floor to Eric's father and heartily greet him, shaking his hand. Abbie and Eric's littlest sister, Merry, shyly approached Lily, likely asking her to play tea party. Lily's bright curls bobbed up and down as the three walked off holding hands, while Hannah's grandfather took a seat across from her father and engaged him in lively conversation.

Occasionally, both men let out bursts of laughter, bringing attention their way. Soon Hannah's parents joined them, and Eric felt his bride slip her hand against the back of his shoulder in relief at their public show of acceptance. As the evening elapsed, the circle increased, others slowly drifting over to meet the father of the groom and his wife, who now sat beside him.

Hannah gripped Eric's arm suddenly. "Look."

He turned. Clemmie's parents moved across the floor, somewhat stiffly, Charleigh clutching her husband's arm. He stood a little taller than Eric's father and had a stronger build; Eric knew Stewart had always been Charleigh's protector. The man looked the part. Brent and Darcy, who were both amazing and never showed any hesitance in accepting Hannah's choice for a husband, also walked with them. It still stunned Eric how much Brent and his father-in-law looked alike, almost twins, and Darcy's brash ways often made him smile.

Both couples now approached Eric Sr., and Hannah tugged on Eric's arm.

"I've got to hear this."

So did Eric.

They moved to the outside of the growing circle, unobserved, an amazing feat since they'd been constantly greeted and pulled every which way since their arrival.

Eric's father, upon seeing the approaching four guests, slowly stood to his feet.

"Charleigh." His voice seemed a little hoarse as he nodded to her. "You look lovely, as always. . .Stewart." The two men shared an unfathomable look before Eric's father turned his gaze to the other couple. "Darcy. Brent. I'm glad you came."

Eric knew his father's words involved more than the wedding.

"You look like the years have been good to you."

Eric wondered if he was the only one who noticed Stewart's dry tone.

"I've been richly blessed." Eric's father reached for his mother's hand and helped her up to stand beside him. His father was a strong man, but Eric sensed his need for her support as he watched him slip an arm around her waist. "It's God who's been good to me. Not the years."

His quiet statement seemed to ease the tension, and Stewart nodded as if he understood what his old nemesis didn't say.

The ice melted, if not broken, Eric's father invited them to join their circle, explaining that they talked of mission days. Eric Jr. knew the subject was sure to interest Hannah's aunts and uncles since they ran a children's reformatory that Hannah said was more of a home for troubled orphans with a need to be loved. After hesitating slightly, both couples sat down.

"Thank God." Eric breathed the prayer in relief, sensing the hardest summit had at last been breached.

"Uh-oh." The sudden nervousness in Hannah's voice caught his attention. She looked across the room. "Um," she giggled. "There's something I forgot to tell you about Joel."

"Oh?"

"He developed a sort of. . .tradition with some of the boys at the Refuge, his gang. He was their leader, and well, I think we're about to become their next victims."

"What?"

At his confusion, she turned him around by the arms to look.

Joel and his buddy Herbert, who'd also become a good friend of Eric's, stood in a line with three other men, their arms linked around each other's shoulders.

"That's Clint with the brown hair, Tommy in the middle, and Lance at the end," Hannah informed him with a resigned grin. "They were childhood buddies at the Refuge, who later called themselves 'The Reformers.' We're about to be serenaded."

"Serenaded?"

The most horrendous screech came from a harmonica Tommy put to his lips to gain the attention of those not already looking their way. Eric winced, and Hannah giggled. "They really do sound better than that."

Eric felt red wash his face as the five friends let loose with a corny ballad of love and longing intended to embarrass the happy couple and wish them well. The crowning moment was when Joel dropped to one knee, holding his hands over his heart, then spreading them wide, as one by one the others followed suit.

"You've just been officially accepted into the fold," Hannah said after the last dying note, a pleased grin on her face. "They only do that for those they consider family."

"Then I guess I should feel flattered." Right now all he felt was embarrassed.

She let out a soft gasp. "Oh Eric, look."

His gaze went back to the circle, which to his surprise had grown larger. Two of his younger siblings sat near his parents' feet, and his father held Eric's youngest brother, Gerard, in his lap. Everyone listened as Eric Sr. related a humorous story, receiving smiles and chuckles all around.

Hannah grasped his arm with both hands, nestling her head against his shoulder. "I think we're going to be all right."

"Non, mon amour, we're going to be better than all right." He looked down into her eyes, and she reached up to give him a kiss, the absolute joy glowing from her face a sight to behold.

After almost three decades involving peril, fear, pain, and regret—redemption and forgiveness had finally, completely visited their households, as Hannah's family opened their circle to the Fontaines. . .and God proved once again that nothing was impossible for Him.

epilogue

"Come in, come in!" Hannah eagerly herded the newest arrivals into her home. "Brrr. It's freezing out there! Let me take your coats."

Her father-in-law kissed her cheeks then shook the snow off his coat before handing it to Hannah. Her mother-in-law moved forward, embracing her. "Hello, dear, you look lovely as always."

Hannah thanked her, taking her coat as well. "The others are in front of the fire in the parlor getting warm."

"Where do I put these?"

Eric's sixteen-year-old brother, Stefan, held what looked like a mountain of presents. He was followed by his seventeen-year-old sister, Lynnette, holding little Gerard's hand, then a giggling Merry, and the rest until all nine children stood inside, and Hannah gratefully closed the door.

"Oh my! It looks like Christmas here already. What did you do?" she laughingly accused her in-laws. "On the coffee table is fine," she told Stefan, who struggled to hold the stack.

Excited to hold her first family gathering, the first time she'd felt well enough for any sort of party, Hannah smiled. Usually they met for cozy gatherings at her parents', at her great-uncle's, at the mission, or at the Refuge.

She addressed the Fontaine children. "Why don't you join the others in the kitchen? Abbie made hot cocoa and cookies for everyone."

Eagerly they nodded and hurried away. She grinned, wondering if her cozy little kitchen would hold them all.

"Eric, good to see you." Uncle Stewart moved across the room to shake his hand. "This weather is for the Eskimos."

"It is, but I couldn't miss my granddaughter's coming out—so, where is she?"

Aunt Charleigh laughed and moved forward to hug him. "Patience never was your strong suit."

"Non," Eric Sr. admitted sheepishly. "You know me too well, ma chère."

In past months after such a personal remark involving the old life, delivered in haste and without thought, an awkward silence followed. Her father-in-law had once conned Aunt Charleigh into believing they were married, so the two had been close at one point in their lives.

Hannah felt relieved to hear her aunt's teasing answer of, "We *all* know you better than you think, Eric Fontaine!"

He stared in mock concern. "Does that mean I'm in trouble?"

"Only if you don't turn around and wish me well, Guv'ner." Aunt Darcy came up behind him from the direction of the kitchen, where she'd left two of her scrumptious berry pies.

He swung around and returned her exuberant embrace. "You've gotten thinner," she chided, pulling away and looking him over with a critical eye. "Keeping too busy at the mission, I'll warrant."

"You're so right, Darcy," Hannah's mother-in-law agreed. "I constantly need to remind him to rest or eat."

"One of your famous pies should do the trick." Hannah's father-in-law gave her aunt a hopeful grin as Uncle Brent appeared from the kitchen with a slice of said pie in hand.

"I call foul," Eric Sr. complained jovially. "The celebration hasn't even started."

Aunt Darcy's eyes twinkled as she moved to Uncle Brent's side and slipped her hand through his arm. "Aye, but he's my husband. He gets special privileges."

Hannah laughed along with the others, grateful the mood hadn't faltered at her father-in-law's slip of the tongue with Charleigh. Clearly enough time had passed, with God's touch, to heal even the deep wounds of decades before.

Her parents entered from the dining room, followed by her grandfather and Great-Uncle Bernard, and greetings were once more exchanged all around. The doorbell rang again, and Hannah answered, relieved to see Clemmie and Joel at last.

"Oh, it's so good to see you." Awkwardly she hugged her dearest friend, then threw her arms around Joel's neck. "I was getting worried."

"I wasn't going to come," Clemmie admitted. "I feel as big as a house with this one." She groaned in laughter, putting a hand to her protruding stomach.

"Unh-uh." Joel's eyes twinkled as he set down their little girl with a kiss to her temple, pulling off her coat, then moving to help his wife out of hers. "Make that two."

Clemmie looked at him grimly, and Joel laughed, dropping a kiss to her nose.

"I wasn't teasing when I said twins run in my family, darling. I really think this could be it."

Hannah didn't voice her opinion, but for once, she didn't think Joel was being mischievous. Clemmie wasn't due for two months and already looked past due. "Hi, Rebecca," Hannah greeted their small, redheaded daughter, who with her fair skin and the outside cold looked as if roses bloomed in her cheeks. The child smiled shyly.

"Where's Eric?" Joel asked, handing her their coats.

"That's a good question. I'll just put these away and see what's keeping him."

Leaving the pleasant buzz of conversation and occasional hearty laughter of her guests behind, Hannah hurried to deposit all the coats on their bed, then went to the nursery, certain she knew where to find her husband.

She paused at the doorway, her heart melting with love to see Eric bent over the cradle, his finger caressing their tiny daughter's cheek.

". . .And that's my side of the family. On your mother's side, there's your Grandma Sarah, who's also a princess, and Grandpa Bill. Your Great-Grandpa Josiah and Great-Uncle Bernard. . .Esther, Abbie, David, Josiah, and Aunt Darcy and Uncle Brent, and all their children. . ."

Hannah grinned, moving forward. "As big as our family is, you'll confuse the poor child."

"Non, she's smart. Do you see how her eyes are lit up with interest?"

"And you're not the least bit biased."

"Is it my fault if we have the most beautiful and intelligent child on the planet?"

Hannah laughed and moved into her husband's arms, lifting her lips to receive his kiss. He held her close, and she sighed in satisfaction, her ear pressed against his chest and the steady beats of his heart.

"They've all arrived."

He sighed. "So I guess that means I should let you go?"

"Never."

For several precious moments, they stood lost in one another, sharing in the joy of their little girl and enclosed in their serene world, while outside the door the laughter and conversation of their loved ones rose and fell like a comforting wave surrounding them.

"They'll wonder where we are," Hannah said after a while.

"*Oui, ma belle princesse.*" With another little sigh, he released her. Carefully, he picked up their tiny daughter, who'd inherited her father's flame blue eyes and Hannah's dimpled smile. Giving their child a kiss on her rosy cheek, he handed her to Hannah.

She smiled at her husband. "Time for her big debut."

"And she'll outshine any starlet ever born."

Hannah laughed as together they moved into the parlor. At their entrance, the family quieted, many gathering around, all looking with eager expectation at the swaddled bundle in her arms. She smiled, and Eric rested his hand upon her shoulder.

"Mothers, fathers, aunts, uncles, cousins, and friends, may we introduce you to Erica Rose Fontaine. . . ."

To her husband's announcement, Hannah silently added, *The precious link that now bonds our families and has helped to make us whole.*

A Letter To Our Readers

Dear Reader:
In order that we might better contribute to your reading
enjoyment, we would appreciate your taking a few minutes
to respond to the following questions. We welcome your
comments and read each form and letter we receive. When
completed, please return to the following:

Fiction Editor
Heartsong Presents
PO Box 719
Uhrichsville, Ohio 44683

1. Did you enjoy reading *In Search of Serenity* by Pamela Griffin?
   ❏ Very much! I would like to see more books by this author!
   ❏ Moderately. I would have enjoyed it more if

   _____

   _____

   _____

2. Are you a member of **Heartsong Presents**? ❏ Yes ❏ No
   If no, where did you purchase this book? _____

   _____

3. How would you rate, on a scale from 1 (poor) to 5 (superior),
   the cover design? _____

4. On a scale from 1 (poor) to 10 (superior), please rate the
   following elements.

   ____ Heroine   ____ Plot
   ____ Hero   ____ Inspirational theme
   ____ Setting   ____ Secondary characters

5. These characters were special because? _____
_____
_____

6. How has this book inspired your life? _____
_____
_____

7. What settings would you like to see covered in future
   Heartsong Presents books? _____
_____
_____

8. What are some inspirational themes you would like to see
   treated in future books? _____
_____
_____

9. Would you be interested in reading other **Heartsong
   Presents** titles?   ❏ Yes   ❏ No

10. Please check your age range:
     ❏ Under 18   ❏ 18-24
     ❏ 25-34   ❏ 35-45
     ❏ 46-55   ❏ Over 55

Name _____
Occupation _____
Address _____
City, State, Zip _____
E-mail _____

WINDY CITY BRIDES

3 stories in 1

There couples rely on faith and love to get them through the adventures and dangers surrounding pivotal moments in Chicago history.

Historical, paperback, 352 pages, 5¾₆" x 8"

Presents

Great Inspirational Romance at a Great Price!

Heartsong Presents books are inspirational romances in contemporary and historical settings, designed to give you an enjoyable, spirit-lifting reading experience. You can choose wonderfully written titles from some of today's best authors like Wanda E. Brunstetter, Mary Connealy, Susan Page Davis, Cathy Marie Hake, Joyce Livingston, and many others.

When ordering quantities less than six, above titles are $3.99 each.
Not all titles may be available at time of order.